Naan the Wiser

A Laughing Loaf Bakery Mystery

Victoria Kazarian

Cover design by Mariah Sinclair

To my father,
Stanley Vierk, who taught me how to play chess.

Chapter One

It was 7:20 a.m. that warm August morning, and we were just about to open the bakery doors.

I looked out the front windows and saw River Grove residents on the sidewalk, already wearing shorts, tank tops, and flip flops on what was predicted to be the hottest day of the summer so far. Hot for our little mountain town, anyway. Ninety degrees.

After setting out the bakery's joke of the day on the front counter, I went into the back room.

Laughing Loaf Joke of the Day
I left my sandwich in the elevator at work.
I wanted to take my lunch to the next level.

We'd been serving lunch at The Laughing Loaf Bakery for a little over a month now—with a newly hired lunch crew and a sandwich, wrap, and salad line. Now my staff and I were working on a new offering, just in time for our catering gig at the first ever River Grove Chess Tournament.

Beck and my Irish bread baker, Maeve, stood over the grill portion of the stove as Beck slid a spatula under an oblong, flattened sandwich.

"Beck, I don't think you put enough butter on that." Maeve peered over Beck's shoulder, scrutinizing her process in preparing our newest sandwich—the *naanini,* made from Indian naan bread. "You can't be stingy with that stuff. That's where the flavor comes from."

Beck set down the spatula and reached for a block of butter. She sliced off a chunk and spread it over the top naan bread's surface and on the grill. Then she pressed the long flat sandwich into the melted butter with the spatula.

"You have to make sure the surface isn't too hot," Maeve said as she watched. "You better flip it right *now*. You don't want that butter to burn."

"Maeve, I know the naan is your baking project, but trust me, I know how to grill." Beck said it sweetly, since this is Beck we're talking about. But anyone who knew my assistant manager could see her patience was being pushed to the limit.

Beck pressed down on the sandwich, then carefully slid another long spatula under the sandwich and lifted it, then carefully turned it upside down. The top was golden brown. Melted cheese seeped out of the sides of the sandwich. Even at the next table, I inhaled a whiff of buttery, toasted flavor.

"Oh, my God!" Rose exclaimed from the metal table where she was cutting beignet dough into squares. "Melted cheese and butter--the best smell there is."

"Samples coming up, once we've got a few of these babies off the grill," Maeve said, as she went back to her spot at the industrial mixer.

A naanini is a similar to panini, the Italian grilled and

pressed sandwich. But it's made with naan, traditional Indian flatbread. Last month, Maeve and I had eaten at an Indian restaurant in Santa Cruz. The naan we'd eaten had become an obsession with us, and we stayed late a few nights at the bakery to perfect our version and experiment with using it for a grilled sandwich. For the filling, we'd settled on sliced chicken and a mild cheese with mint chutney. With a side of raita, the Indian yogurt dip, for dipping.

We'd introduce the naanini just in time for River Grove's first annual chess tournament—to be held at The Riverside Saloon. Our tie-in was that the game of chess actually originated in India.

When my dad, retired physics professor Dr. John Markley, met The Riverside's owner, Reggie McFerrin, they bonded over their love of the game. Whenever they played chess or engaged in casual conversation about it, Reggie and my dad disappeared into their own private world, recounting games they'd played, move by move, in a kind of shared reverie.

I was glad they had each other for this obsession, a sentiment my dad's girlfriend Mary Jo shared. She was happy for his interest but would sooner put a knitting needle through her eye than play a game of it. I recognized the glazed look in her eyes when my dad started explaining in detail a brilliant opening move he'd studied from a world champion.

Still, I had grown up playing chess with my dad, and I was excited about the tournament.

For one, it was something new and exciting happening in our little town. I was proud of my dad for organizing it. He was becoming more and more woven into the fabric of River Grove which—thanks to the federal witness protection program, WITSEC—had become our home.

Reggie and my dad had invited ten highly ranked

players from the West Coast to participate. They would descend on The Riverside on Labor Day weekend for games, dinners, mingling, and local sightseeing. They'd play Friday, Saturday, and Sunday, then finish up on Monday morning.

For that Monday, Reggie and my father had also opened up space for any chess players in the area to come play during a community tournament in the afternoon. My bird-photographer boyfriend Nate Behrens agreed to play during this time.

Nate enjoyed my dad and didn't mind playing chess with him, despite being beaten each time. It was the loud crowing my dad did after he won that grated on his nerves.

One afternoon last month, not long after we'd reopened the newly remodeled Laughing Loaf, Reggie had come over to talk with Beck and me. He had a proposition.

"Gracie, if you're taking on catering gigs again, I'd like to have The Laughing Loaf cater lunches for the tournament. You can do a buffet, or you can have servers making sandwiches like you do here. Whatever you think would work best, Gracie."

I frowned across the table at Reggie, puzzled.

"But you already have an excellent chef. Chef Jorge's already on site. Why would you want The Laughing Loaf to do lunch?"

Reggie smiled. Or at least his mouth smiled. I couldn't see his eyes behind the mirrored aviator glasses he wore indoors and out.

"You offer something different. Your bread and baked goods are better than what we have at The Riverside. Besides, it would take a huge effort to rearrange our staff shifts for three days in order to serve lunch at noon. I'm really hoping this works for your schedule."

I thought about how we'd do this. Thankfully, I'd hired four new employees last month; the extra hands were turning out to be very helpful. We'd need to staff the lunch line at the bakery and send a lunch crew over to The Riverside for three days.

"I think we can do this, Reggie. It's always better to make things fresh." I looked across the table at Beck, who gave me a subtle nod. "I'll work with the staff to get servers on board and come up with a plan."

"I'd appreciate that, Gracie." Reggie said. "I've got a few thoughts for the menu. But we can talk when we get closer to that weekend."

I was thrilled about the prospect of catering the tournament, meeting the players and watching some matches.

The catering gig immediately sparked Beck's creativity. She'd drawn a few sketches, one of them a checkerboard cake topped with chocolate chess pieces. Our naanini, once we figured out how to keep it hot and fresh, would be a great menu offering. Beck, along with Rose, one of my newer hires, wanted to add chai tea to our drinks menu and were already working on a recipe to make it from scratch.

After talking to our lunch servers, I decided it would be smart to ask Chloe Westerman, our police chief's granddaughter, if she could help us that weekend. She'd taken a summer job with the River Grove Recreation Department, but it was only on weekdays, so she would be able to work at the bakery from Saturday morning on. This would help a lot.

Especially with what would end up happening at the tournament.

. . .

AFTER THE STAFF left that evening, I went to get my dog Biga, who'd been lounging in our air-conditioned bakery all day. His pen was in a small room off the bakery's back room. He lifted his head and gave me a weary look: *Finally.*

"We get to go home! Aren't you thrilled? No working A/C, but lots of box fans set up by our in-house physicist to channel air flow. It won't be so bad."

Biga went into his crate willingly. I slipped my tote bag and purse over my arm, picked up the crate, and shut down the lights and locked up. Nate was coming over to barbecue for my dad and me tonight, which got me off the hook for making dinner. I'd also get to see him, since the bakery had had been crazy busy since our reopening. I wanted to cuddle with him on the porch swing and relax for the evening.

After my busy day and the heat outside, I'd probably just fall asleep on him, but that was fine with me.

WHEN WE GOT HOME, my dad was drinking a cold beer in his recliner, while scrolling through a spreadsheet of player statistics for the tournament.

My dad had set up the fans well today—the house was a comfortable temperature, and there was a gentle breeze circulating. I released Biga and he made a run for my dad, jumping up into the recliner and settling right in front of my father's laptop screen. My dad picked up the laptop and set it on the arm of the chair, while continuing to cuddle Biga.

"Nate'll be here at six. I've got the salmon marinating in the fridge. Did you make the salad?"

My father's eyes widened as he checked the time on his

watch. He closed his laptop. "Ah, *no*, but I will. Reggie and I are finalizing player pairings for the tournament. I must have lost track of time—"

"Hey, I get it," I said with an affectionate smile. "This is a big deal. And it's next week."

My dad stood up, and he and Biga followed me back to the kitchen. He pulled bags of produce out of the fridge, while I filled Biga's food and water bowl. My boy noisily lapped from his bowl, so the heat must have been getting to him.

"Reggie's meeting with us Tuesday to do some tasting and go over final arrangements for lunch. I'm getting excited, too. Beck's working on a chess-themed dessert with dark chocolate and white chocolate that's going to be stunning."

I took plates out and began setting our small dining room table for dinner. Something had been bugging me, something I wanted to ask my dad about. But it had been a busy day at the bakery and my mind was mush. I kept trying to remember what it was.

I took off my purse and set it down on the counter. I saw my burner phone poking out. I'd been keeping it near me in case I needed to call the federal agents assigned to us in WITSEC. Earlier this summer, we had a run-in with some European dissidents and a very nosy employee.

Then it came to me.

"Dad, all the players in the tournament are from the West Coast, right? Are any of them from Seattle?"

My dad had launched into salad prep and was now slicing carrots with extreme precision, as usual. At first, I thought he hadn't heard me. Then he laid down the knife and looked up.

"Not at this time. But we just had a competitor back out

—a young man from San Jose. Reggie and I are looking for another player to fill the spot. I believe we have some names from the Pacific Northwest on the list. One of them sounds familiar, but it could simply be a common name."

Since my father and I had gone into witness protection, after I turned in my tech-spy husband to the FBI, I sometimes got a little paranoid. We'd been relocated from Seattle, where my father taught physics at the University.

"What if someone from up there recognizes you? What if our cover is blown?"

My dad landed on the side of being completely oblivious. Unlike me, he was an optimist by nature. The gears in his head were spinning away, thinking of things like Einstein's theory of relativity or replaying a series of chess moves. He wasn't stressed about foreign spies discovering us, though that fear *had* become reality just a month ago.

It was always fresh in my mind.

"The probability of that seems quite low, my dear," my father said, as he peeled a cucumber. "I think you worry too much."

"I need to remind you." I took a deep breath. "Some of the things I worry about have actually happened."

I heard a familiar knock on the front door, and it made my heart beat faster.

"Our griller is here," I said with a smile, and I got up to get the door. Biga beat me to it since he knew exactly who was here.

I looked out the peephole to make sure this wasn't an imposter, then opened the door. Nate was standing there, a serious look on his face, his bag of grilling paraphernalia strapped across his chest. Like a barbecue desperado, armed and ready. His lips twitched as he tried to resist the impulse to smile.

"Your chef reporting for duty, and I'm ready to heat things up."

I turned red and giggled.

"My dad's in the kitchen making salad," I said in a whisper.

Nate bent down and gave me a long, deep kiss. Not exactly a pre-dinner appetizer.

I'm glad he put his arm around me because my knees started to buckle, and I almost fell over.

"Let me escort you to the grill," I said, recovering my balance. "The salmon's been marinating all afternoon. I'll bring it out."

Biga followed us out—or rather followed Nate, whom he seemed to like a lot more than me tonight. Probably because Nate was in charge of the food.

The grill was immaculate since he'd cleaned it after our last barbecue. He opened the lid and turned it on, igniting the flame.

I brought out the salmon, some veggies I'd skewered, and a cold beer for each of us.

"Nice." Nate used a bottle opener to open our drinks and handed me mine. "I've been cleaning out my photo shed all day, and I realize I need to bite the bullet and install A/C if this weather keeps up. It was like a sauna in there today."

Nate photographed wildlife, mostly birds, for a living. He'd set up a darkroom and a computer for digital editing in the shed next to his house. Beck and her husband Sam lived next door to Nate—Sam had helped him with the renovation.

Nate held the bottle up and took a big gulp.

"It'll be worth it for you, trust me. The bakery is so much better after we got air conditioning last summer."

Nate deftly wielded a grilling spatula to flip a salmon filet on the grill. He grimaced. "I need to call about that tomorrow. Along with everyone else who's waited this long."

My dad poked his head out the back door. "Hello, Nate. I'm wondering if we should eat inside. It's still awfully hot out here."

I pressed my cold beer bottle to my face. "Yes, *please.*"

"Let's do it." Nate nodded.

When the salmon was ready, Nate took the filets off the grill and stacked them on the platter I'd brought out. When the skewered veggies had gotten a nice char, he pulled them off the grill and plated them.

We went inside, where my dad had set the salad and a pitcher of ice water on the table with lemon slices floating in it. With the roasted salmon and vegetables and the lemony scent, the room smelled like summer. Summer has never been my favorite season, but times like this, gathering together over grilled food, were the highlight of the season for me.

"Nice touch with the lemon slices," I grinned at my dad, who was laying out silverware. "Very posh."

"Mary Jo suggested it." The warm look in his eyes when he said her name was sweet. "She said it tastes more refreshing."

I poured us all glasses of the lemon water and sat down.

Nate must have been hungry since his salmon filet was almost gone. I knew he'd ridden his bike down to Aptos on the coast this morning. He probably needed his calories.

"John, who's the favorite to win the tournament?" He ate his last bite, then took a gulp of cold beer.

"Our highest ranked player is Andrew Mehta. Just graduated from college in San Diego." My father drank some lemon water. "He's starting to play in bigger tournaments now and is getting a lot of attention. Of course, you never know. We have some up-and-coming players. We're doing a Swiss round system. Nobody is eliminated, and the winner is determined by total points after the last match."

"Are you and Reggie just running things or will you get a chance to play later?" Nate sat back, finished with his food.

I would imagine my dad would jump at the chance to play someone like Mehta, since he had such an easy time playing anyone else in River Grove—with the exception of Reggie, that is.

My dad swallowed a gulp of cool ale. "Reggie is the tournament director since he's qualified by the US Chess Federation. But on Labor Day, the two of us might take on some of the champions in informal games. I don't know that I'd beat any of them, but I'd enjoy the challenge."

He sat there, fork poised over his salmon, a dreamy smile on his face, as if he were considering the idea right now.

"I read an article about Mehta," Nate said. "One of the chess magazines said his opening moves are smart. *A lightning-quick path to checkmate* was the way I heard it described. It's based on setting traps for his opponents. He lures them in by putting a piece out there that looks like an easy catch."

My dad lit up like a fireplace full of embers. "Yes! It's actually not uncommon, but he plans his strategies quite well. I've been thinking about how I'd counter them if I were to play him. If I'm going to do that, I need to do my homework."

My dad went on in detail to describe some of Mehta's typical opening moves. My mind immediately began to drift

—thinking about anything else but chess: how to perfect our naanini process and get the hot sandwiches over to The Riverside while they were at their freshest. And what other cookie or treat we could add to our dessert line for the tournament.

I'd grown up being my dad's in-house chess partner, always available for games, but chess was not really my passion.

But there Nate was, listening intently, asking my dad questions about Mehta's strategy and showing he knew chess at a higher level than I did.

My dad responded to it eagerly, running to get a pencil and paper so he could diagram a series of moves to try.

My dad adored Nate, and if he were to become his son-in-law someday, my dad would be thrilled. Though he was careful not to give opinions about that, since he felt that his approval, as parental approval sometimes does, might push me away from Nate. My ex-husband Ben certainly hadn't been a great addition to the family. He wasn't capable of seeing past himself to care about anyone else's interests.

On the other hand, Nate genuinely enjoyed my dad and took pains to show him respect, even though my father could be a bit much sometimes. It made me wonder what Nate's own father had been like; his parents had died in a plane crash when Nate was eighteen. He didn't talk much about them.

My dad eagerly showed Nate the diagram of the opening moves, but he didn't push it. Nate nodded and said that he'd never seen this approach in a chess game. After an intense discussion about the importance of the knight piece, my father started clearing our dishes and loading the dishwasher.

I set out a plate of red and black checkerboard refrigerator cookies, based on the checkerboard cookies my mother used to make when I was growing up. I'd used gel colors to make them the colors of a vintage chess board, black and red checks.

"These are cool." Nate eagerly grabbed a couple.

"Nate, I appreciate you cooking tonight, especially with the heat," my father said, closing the dishwasher to run it. "Once I finish up here, I'll be in my study, working on tournament business. I'll be out of your way."

When my father finished up and went down the hall to his study, Nate looked at me, a sly grin on his face.

"How often do we get this room to ourselves?" He laughed like a supervillain and rubbed his hands together. "He won't be presiding over us from his recliner."

I snorted. "He might be getting some coaching from Mary Jo. He's been good with the social cues tonight. Even thanking you. I mean, what's with that?"

With our delicious freedom, we convened to the sofa in the living room for a few minutes, for some light snogging and of course, some time playing with Biga, who was excited that his second-favorite person was paying attention to him (his favorite being Reggie).

As we saw the sun sink lower through the window in a show of deep pink and orange, Nate sat up.

"It's already feeling cooler. Want to go for a walk? I love this time of the evening."

"Me, too." We stood up and I went to find my sneakers. Biga knew something was up. He looked between the two of us to see if he was going to be part of this.

"You already made the decision for us," I said, chiding Nate. "He heard you say the W word. He's excited and ready to go." I looked over to see Biga already on his way to the door.

"I have no problem with him going along with us." Nate looked down at Biga affectionately. "The guy's been cooped up in the bakery all day."

I called back to my dad that we'd be out walking.

I went to get the leash and harness from the hook in the kitchen. Biga was beside himself now, scampering to the door then back to me. It took a while for him to settle down so I could put his harness on and snap on his leash.

As always, Biga was thrilled to be going outside with us. But there was something different about Nate tonight. A certain look in his eye. He really wanted to get out of the house with me. I studied his face as we went outside.

I'd wait to see what this was about.

Chapter Two

We slipped out of the front door into the cooler evening air, scented with jasmine from the bushes in our front yard. The still-warm evening held me close like a hug.

One thing I loved about summer in River Grove is how it rewards you for making it through a hot day. The air cools, a breeze rises up, and everyone can finally enjoy being outside without feeling like a roasted chicken. Tonight, I smelled the river, the grass and jasmine bushes in our backyard, and the carpet of pine needles along the riverbank; the heat had released their rich fragrances throughout the day and the breezes carried them our way now.

We walked down to the end of our street, Pilgrim Way, to see the San Luciano River

lapping at the rocks along the shore. The water level was down, since it was summer, but there'd been enough rains earlier this year to keep the river flowing. Kids waded in the shallow water, splashing each other. One toddler fell down, landing abruptly on her bottom. She looked around, anguished, until she saw her dad, then lifted her arms for him as she laughed with relief.

I led Biga along the path, until Nate bent down and picked up a flat, smooth rock.

"Perfect skipping rock," I said. "Let me find one."

He poked around in the dirt near the shore, and found a smooth, flat one a few feet away. He handed it to me. "This should work."

Once we were away from the children splashing, he stood on the shore, squatted, then threw his rock in a level, clean throw across the water.

It skipped three times before it landed with a plunk near the far side of the river.

"That was a very graceful throw." I leaned into him with an arm around his waist. "I'm not going to be able to do anywhere near that."

"C'mon." He grinned and took Biga's leash from me. "I bet you can."

I fitted the smooth rock between my thumb and fore-finger and squatted like he did so I could throw the rock level across the water.

I thrust it in a kind of sideways toss, with a snap of my wrist.

Then I stood and watched in amazement.

It bounced two, three, then four times across the water's surface then plunked into the water satisfyingly. When its fancy show was over, it had landed under an overhanging branch from the opposite shore.

I'm not sure I knew what I was doing; I'd just tried to stand and throw like Nate had.

Nate gave me a look of admiration. "*Somebody's* been practicing."

"That was my first good skip ever." I stood up, feeling

pretty proud of myself. Could I do it again? I searched the ground for another rock. I picked up one that wasn't perfectly flat, but it should do okay.

Nate bent down and scoured the shore, trying to find a rock for himself. Biga looked like he was pawing around helping him, until I realized he was starting to do his poop dance, circling around till he was perfectly positioned for a drop.

"Watch out, Biga's ready to do his thing. There are bags in the pouch on his leash."

Biga did his thing, and Nate waited patiently with a bag ready to pick it up. He did and gingerly carried it over to the trash receptacle and dropped it in. On the way back to the shore, with a relieved Biga, he spotted a rock.

"Okay, Biga. Now to see if I can up my skipping game. What do you think?" He bent down and showed the rock to Biga, who sniffed it.

Biga gave Nate a skeptical look, as if to say:
Why are you so excited? This isn't even food.

Nate aligned himself and bent down then tossed his rock. It skipped four times over a patch of smooth, slow-moving river water.

I got my rock ready in my hand. The pressure was on now. I had to bump this up to five skips. "It's *on*."

Not that I'm competitive or anything.

I squatted and tried to throw the same level way I had before. But the magic that had enabled me to achieve my glorious four-point-skip was gone. Maybe it was the imperfect rock. It made one sad, unceremonious *thunk* into the water.

Nate snickered and came over to me, Biga in tow.

"Your four-skip throw was very impressive," he said, hugging me.

The family a few yards up the river from us was getting ready to leave, with the exception of one curly headed little boy, who refused to get out of the water. He was squealing and making big splashes with his arms on the water. Practically daring his dad to come fish him out.

"I don't blame him," I said, as Nate and I sat down on a large rock on the shore. "It's so nice and cool out here. Who wants to go back to a hot house?"

Nate put a hand on my arm. "Look at the sky," he said, staring upwards. "There's still the pink, but now you can see the stars trying to take over, even though they're still faint. The sunset has to give in to the night at some point, but it's taking its time. It's a show off."

The tree branches, silhouetted dark against the pink sky, looked like a piece of fine black lace.

"Summer in River Grove isn't so bad," I said, leaning into him, feeling the electricity of his bare arm on mine.

His voice was soft and rough at the same time. "It's the place I never knew I wanted to be."

"Seattle was all I ever knew. But this feels like home now. In a deeper way."

Nate reached for my hand.

We sat for a while, while Biga tugged on the leash and looked up at us impatiently. Finally, with an exasperated glance, he gave up. He lay down in the warm dirt and put his head down.

Nate pointed at a black bird sitting very still on the branch of a tree across the river. His face suddenly became soft, and his lips curved up in a smile, as it did whenever he spotted a bird.

"Is that a crow?" I asked.

Nate angled his head toward the branch across the water. "It's a raven. See? You can see him shimmer if he catches the light just right. Their feathers are iridescent, and a crow's are not. If he flies, watch for the shape of his tail. Ravens have more wedge-shaped tail feathers."

"He's not a bad omen or anything? He looks spooky. Like he's watching us."

"Probably not a sign of bad luck. He's just enjoying his evening like we are." Nate squeezed my hand affectionately and laughed. He planted a kiss on my forehead. "I mean, cut the bird some slack, Gracie." I gave him a playful punch in the shoulder.

Enough had already happened in River Grove without a black bird telegraphing that trouble was on its way.

"I've never gotten any convenient heads-up before bad things have happened in my life, come to think of it."

"That would be helpful." Nate snorted. "Not that I would have really listened to it anyway." But there was something in his tone, and I could tell this was enough talk of hard things for him.

He let go of my hand and stood up. "Why don't we walk down to the clearing? It'll be a great spot to see the moon tonight."

I slid down off the rock and joined him. Biga looked up at us, relieved that we boring humans were actually going to do something.

"Let's get down there before it gets too dark." Nate started to jog. Biga, with Nate holding his leash, took him up on his challenge. I trailed behind, my feet pounding on the slightly damp trail. Running was so not my thing.

As we headed down the trail, lights began to turn on in houses along the way. In the few backyards along the trail, parents relaxed in chairs enjoying the now-cooler evening. Children ran around, releasing a last burst of energy before bedtime.

Within ten minutes, we entered the deep forested section of the trail, where it turned away from the river, just before downtown. The temperature dropped and the canopy of branches above hid the last traces of sunset.

"It's been a while since I've walked the trail from our house," I said, catching up and taking Biga's leash from Nate. "It would take me longer, but I could walk home with Biga at lunch sometimes, when I need to drop him off with my dad."

"It's what—three miles or so?" Nate turned around to look at me.

"It would be good exercise for both of us. Biga would love it."

Soon we were on the section of trail parallel to downtown, and I saw the dining balcony of The Riverside Saloon, outlined in strings of bright white lights. The tables were full, and as we passed, a few people eating appetizers and drinking cool beverages waved at us.

"Hey, Gracie!"

"Nice homer with the River Rats last Friday, Nate!"

Nate leaned into me and whispered sheepishly, "Guess I redeemed myself with that run after striking out."

"They would love you anyway. You know that, right?" I wrapped an arm around his waist.

"I do." A faint smile crossed his face. "Therapy's been helping. Who knew it felt so good to open up and talk about things."

He hadn't talked at all about his sessions, which he decided to start a few months ago. He'd experienced the loss of his parents and, more recently, his brother. When I'd taken on crime solving, he'd gotten scared he'd lose me, too.

I knew he'd felt guilt along with the fear, as he thought about his brother Nico's death. But over time I could see him becoming lighter and freer as he talked about feelings he'd never shared.

After The Riverside, the trail moved deeper into the woods, diverging again from the river, till we finally came to the clearing, circled by massive redwoods.

The clearing was a meeting place. A place, strangely, where people chose to do one of two things: make out or meditate.

I often ran into Reggie McFerrin here on my walks with Biga. It wasn't far from The Riverside, and it was where he came to sit and think. The first thing I learned about The Riverside's former-hippie owner was that he was a thoughtful man.

Tonight, the clearing, spread with pine needles that crunched under our feet, smelled rich and fragrant.

Nate turned his gaze to the sky, and I saw his face touched with silvery light.

The moon was suspended over us, unreal in its brightness. It looked like the sky was holding a flashlight to us, like a parent demanding to know what we were doing out here so late.

Nate looked down at me, then pulled me close to him.

"Best place to be right now."

"Best person to *be with*," I shot back at him, wrapping my arms around him. He took my hand and gently spun me around, his dance partner.

I felt a closeness with him that I'd felt many times through the past two years, but it was stronger tonight. I blamed the pull of the moon.

"I don't know how to say these things," he began, clearing his throat. At first, I started to feel sick to my stomach, as if for some reason, he was going to break bad news to me. Over the past few years, I'd gotten a little too used to hearing disappointing news. I was always on guard for it.

"I've never met anyone like you, Gracie. You're brave. And honest. And you have a great sense of humor." The corner of his mouth turned up in a smile. "Obviously, I lived okay for thirty-five years not even knowing you, but I don't want to continue without you." He stared down at the ground and took in a deep breath before he looked up at me and continued.

"Someday, I want to not have to drive back home at night. And I love your father, but I don't want to carry on a relationship with you while he sits there watching from his recliner."

He groaned and did a face palm. "Holy crap. Could I be messing this up any worse?"

I squeezed his hand. "You're not messing anything up."

He looked down at me, a pained expression on his face.

"I want to be with you, Gracie. Just us. Of course, we have jobs that take up a lot of our lives. I'm going to continue to do shoots, with a lot of travel. You're busy running a business. We both love what we do. But I want us to be able to come home to each other. Does that make sense?"

My heart pounded. Was this what I thought it was?

"When you say, just *us*—what does that mean?" I thought of watching the kids play in the river earlier on our walk. So I decided to get bold and ask. I didn't want to take it for granted. I'd done that with Ben for eight years, and it turned out he'd never wanted kids. Ever.

"I don't want to freak you out or anything. But have you ever thought about. . . having kids?"

What if his answer was no? What if he didn't like kids?

I saw his eyes water up. "I've always wanted them. But that's gotta be your call, Gracie."

Soon my eyes were tearing up, too.

"I think I do. Not, like right *now*. But someday. Ben didn't."

Nate studied my face and nodded. "It's not for everyone. And from what I know about Ben, it's probably a good thing you didn't have kids."

In a moment of honesty, I told him about watching Phil Wakeman's kids play their crazy game of baseball with their made-up rules in Grove Park a few months ago when I was looking for clues for another crime at the softball field. It had touched me, made me think it was something I wanted. I'd grown up in a quiet house as the only child of two introverts. I loved both my parents dearly, but I wanted something different: a fun, lively house, full of laughter.

I wanted someone who'd be willing to put up with the messiness of having kids. Who'd play with them and laugh with them in their goofiness and let them be themselves.

Nate raised his eyebrows warily. "The Wakemans? I've seen those kids around town with Phil and his wife on the weekends. They are over-the-top crazy. They never stop. Our kids wouldn't be like that, would they?"

I laughed, filled with a bubbling-over sense of relief. When I talked, it sounded like I was choking.

"They might," I said mischievously.

He pulled me close, laughing.

"We've dealt with a lot worse. Not that kids are easy, but if we wanted to become parents, I think we could handle it."

We walked back slowly in a darkness occasionally lit up by moonlight when the tree branches parted overhead.

Crickets chirped and frogs croaked along the river, and their noise seemed joyful to me.

There was a lightness to our conversation on our walk back. Something we'd been brooding about separately had been brought out into the open and we'd both got answers we wanted. We were giddy with relief. Our conversation was littered with nervous laughter and really bad jokes.

Nothing is for certain. Nothing is guaranteed.

I think that was part of what Nate was dealing with in therapy.

But for the first time in months, I felt a sense of peace. I'd been afraid to think about the future for so long.

Now, I was thinking--maybe it wouldn't be so bad.

We got back late, so after some prolonged cuddling on the front porch, Nate said goodbye, even after Biga tried to climb up his leg to stop him.

I went inside to get some sleep for my 4:30 a.m. wakeup.

We'd meet with Reggie this coming week to touch base on our tournament catering arrangements.

I had my checkerboard cookies ready, and Beck had crafted decorations for the chess cake she'd show Reggie.
Not knowing what would come our way during the Labor Day tournament, my walk with Nate tonight had lightened my mood.
This was going to be *fun*.

Chapter Three

I got to the bakery early the next morning and turned on the lights.

Then I cranked up the music.

My mood called for some upbeat pop, and I had just the playlist for it.

I was mixing brioche in the industrial mixer when Beck came in, her hair piled high on her head, to stay cool in today's heat.

She started smiling as soon as she heard me singing along to the playlist.

"You're either in a really good mood or a bad mood," she said, as she took off her light jacket. "Judging by this music, either you're already happy or you're trying to cheer yourself up."

I nodded. "I'm feeling pretty good. It's supposed to be another hot day, but we've got great A/C here. I had a talk and moonlight walk with Nate last night, which was wonderful. I have *nothing* to complain about."

Beck watched me with amusement as she put on her apron.

"I don't think I've ever seen you like this, Gracie."

I gave her a curious smile. Then what was I like normally? Anxious about spies pursuing me? Preoccupied with solving murders? Probably.

"Really," I said with a chuckle. "Well, enjoy it while it lasts." I shut off the stand mixer, twisted the big bowl off its stand, and lugged it to the metal table.

"Well, I'm happy for you, Gracie." Beck pulled out the baked tart shells and began working on fillings. "For whatever you're happy about."

She had a faint smile on her face, and I think she was hoping I would tell her more.

I dumped the bowl out on the floured surface of the metal table.

"How's the chess cake coming along?"

Beck's eyes lit up. "I made the chess pieces and the chess board squares last night and I think they look pretty good. I molded them out of white and dark chocolate."

I couldn't wait to see the cake fully assembled. Beck's sketch earlier this week looked amazing, and I'd been hoping she'd have time to make it a reality.

"My checkerboard cookies are in the freezer, ready to bake. They're from all old recipe my mom used when I was growing up."

"There's something special about refrigerator cookies." Beck went to work slicing beignet dough. "My brothers and I used to raid the freezer and cut off pieces of the roll to eat. It tasted like ice cream to us. We sure got in trouble, though."

I was sure Beck's mom, who seemed a grim and formidable woman, would not be happy with that.

"How did she punish you?"

"We couldn't have any of the baked cookies. Not *one*." Beck looked up from cutting, her face sober.

"Well, that actually sounds fair." I'd been imagining being grounded for a week or being forced to read the bible in a closet or something.

I'd just put the brioche loaves into the oven, when Maeve and Rose came in, laughing.

"Good morning, Gracie and Beck!" They went to their lockers to put their stuff away, still giggling, then emerged and put on their aprons.

"Maeve has a great story," Rose said, her lips tightened as if she was barely keeping from exploding into a grin, as she pulled out our huge pot for frying beignets.

"You've got to tell us," Beck said, as she piled beignet dough squares onto a parchment-lined tray.

"This salesman came to the door last night around dinner time, while I was making us dinner, so I could hear all this in the next room when Mayor C answered the door. He was selling knives. He had this kit with him, full of his wares, I guess. He asked Corinne if she needed any knives. She asked him, 'Why would I need any knives? Are these knives for self-defense?' And he was really serious when he said timidly, 'No, ma'am. You use them in your kitchen.'"

Rose giggled. Maeve continued.

"And then, she starts firing questions at him. 'What company do you work for? Is this company legitimate or is it a scam? Please show me your credentials. Before you show me knives, I have to see this is an actual company.'

"Then she asks his name—Marco. 'Do you get a percentage of the sales, Marco?' And then she makes this switch from being suspicious to being super sympathetic to the guy's lot in life. 'Do you feel you're being paid fairly, Marco? Is there any room for promotion in your job?'"

I nodded and laughed. "That sounds exactly like Mayor C."

"Then, poor Marco gets really nervous because he's there to sell knives, not tell his whole life story. He says he has to go and starts making excuses. But she kept asking him questions. Finally, from what Mayor C told me, he picked up his knife kit with both hands and made a run for it."

I snorted, as the rest of my staff dissolved into laughter. Maeve was staying at Mayor C's house during the week, and the two got along well. Anyone with less than Maeve's spunk and sense of humor might be intimidated by Mayor C. River Grove's mayor could be a little in-your-face.

"If she's that way with door-to-door salesmen, imagine what she'd do if a burglar ever broke into the house. She'd sit him down and ask him about his life choices," Maeve said, as she got to work making flatbread dough in the industrial mixer. "I feel quite safe."

"I want to stay on Mayor C's good side," Rose said with a smirk. "Imagine what she could do if she used her powers for evil, not good."

Beck didn't usually join in on any joke that was at another person's expense, but I saw her grinning to herself as she took the beignet squares over to the stove.

After I loaded up the display case up front with fresh cinnamon rolls, I set out the joke of the day, thinking of my friend, Elana. She'd love the joke, and I laughed to myself because it reminded me of her.

Laughing Loaf Joke of the Day
The other day, my best friend asked me
to pass her her lipstick.
I accidentally handed her a glue stick.
She still isn't talking to me.

The week of the River Grove Chess Tournament had arrived.

Beck, Maeve, and I had been working hard on preparations for the tournament, making sure everything was ready for Reggie to sample today—and that we'd be prepared for lunch service at The Riverside starting Friday.

We opened that Tuesday at 7:30 a.m. to a small crowd of customers, half of them with laptop bags. Remote workers, most of them employed in the tech industry in Silicon Valley, often chose to get work done at our bakery instead of staying home, probably because of our air conditioning. I couldn't blame them.

As soon as we closed the bakery at 2:30 p.m., I preheated the oven and took out the plastic-wrapped rolls of red-and-black checkerboard refrigerator cookie dough. I cut it into ¼" thick slices and placed them on a cookie sheet. The checkered pattern looked neat and precise and the contrasting colors popped.

I resisted the urge to eat a slice of the cold, sweet dough —mostly because of the risk of salmonella from raw eggs, not because I expected Beck's mom to materialize in the back room and tell me I was forbidden to eat any baked cookies.

The enticing smell of cookies filled the back room, overwhelming even the smell of freshly baked breads.

"Are you sharing those, Gracie?" Maeve asked from where she was putting naan on baking sheets.

"Later. Reggie gets first dibs."

"I'll have naanini ready for him when he comes in. Freshly fried in butter. I'll mix up some of the mint chutney and raita, too."

"Yes, please, Maeve."

Beck had set up a table next to the far wall, to make sure

she had room to decorate the chess cake. She'd baked the pieces for the three layers earlier and they were cooling on racks. She was preparing a crumb coat to keep the layers smooth before frosting them and had a bowl of white buttercream frosting whipped up.

Her piping bag filled with chocolate frosting sat ready. The molded chocolate lay out on a parchment sheet: an elegant, shiny queen in dark chocolate, along with a chocolate pawn, a bishop and a knight. A white chocolate king, a rook and a pawn were grouped together. Stacks of white squares and chocolate squares sat ready to patch together into a board.

Beck stood there, taking in a deep breath. She closed her eyes.

"Beck, what's up?" I asked as I passed behind her on my way to get a cooling rack for my cookies.

She looked worried. "I've done so much already, getting everything set. It's been a lot of work. I'm afraid now I'll mess this up and ruin it all."

I knew how she felt. She'd been working on this for a few days now, practicing and perfecting different parts of the cake, even at home. This would be the display piece for desserts at the tournament. She wanted it to be perfect.

I knew that if Beck finished this, it would be about as close to perfect as one of our desserts could be.

"Even if it's not perfect enough for you, everyone's going to love this," I told her. "Relax and enjoy this. Besides, this is to show Reggie today. Think of this as your dress rehearsal cake."

Beck nodded slowly. "I guess. The problem is, I know what it *can* look like. And I don't want anything less than that."

"Remember, you can learn from this cake and make the one for this weekend perfect. Cut yourself some slack."

She took a breath and sighed. "I guess you're right. I will learn what to look out for on the next one."

With a look of intense focus and determination, Beck picked up her offset spatula and started applying a crumb coat of frosting to the layers of white- and chocolate-checkered cake. I didn't want to make her any more nervous than she was, so I went back to get my fragrant cookies on the cooling racks.

Rose put on a calming indie folk playlist, and I shot her a thankful look. We were all intent on getting things ready for Reggie's visit.

Not that he would be a harsh critic of our work, but we all adored Reggie and were excited about catering the tournament. We wanted to put our best work out there.

At three fifteen, Maeve started up the grill. She laid out two naan and buttered their tops then laid one down and piled it with layers of chicken and Indian paneer cheese. Then she spread the mint chutney over the cheese and laid another buttered naan on top.

She let it sizzle on the grill till the cheese melted, then covered it with a cloche lid to help the cheese and fillings meld together. After a few minutes, she took the cloche off and pressed down on the top naan.

The buttery smell of grilled naan and fragrant spices filled the room.

"You're making me hungry again, Maeve," Rose called from the metal table, where she was mixing more beignet dough.

My stomach rumbled, and the sound was barely covered by Rose's folk playlist. I hoped Maeve was planning on making some more, so we could all share. As usual, I hadn't had time to grab anything to eat for lunch.

A few minutes later, there were three naanini on a plate.

"They're ready," Maeve said as she admired her work. She used a bench scraper to cut two of the sandwiches up into fourths. "Come try some."

Rose and I made our way to the plate and picked up a piece. I bit into the buttery grilled naan, then tasted the spicy middle of the sandwich, with the mint-cilantro of the chutney, the melted cheese, and the sliced chicken. It was a great combination of flavors.

"Delicious, Maeve." I finished off my piece. Maeve specialized in bread, but this was her first menu item, and it was a winner.

"I don't even think you need the yogurt sauce to dip it into." Beck finished off her portion of the sandwich quickly. "It's moist enough without it. Maybe only if people wanted to tone down the spice."

"I think so, too," Maeve said, as she took one last piece of the naanini.

"Let's have the raita dip available, though," I said, thinking that my father couldn't be the only one who'd want relief from the spices.

With the naanini, wraps, salad bar, and desserts, we were pretty much ready for the tournament catering. Elise and Daisy would go over Friday morning to set up the lunch station, while Tyler and Evan ran lunch service at the bakery. Again, I was so glad we had enough staff to handle both sites comfortably over the weekend.

Beck was carefully setting the molded chocolate chess pieces on the squares of her cake, adding a small dollop of frosting on the squares to glue the pieces in place.

She looked very focused, so I passed by her and whispered. "Looks amazing, Beck."

When Reggie came to the back door, I gave him a hug and led him to a table in the front dining area. He smelled, as always, like sandalwood and patchouli. He wasn't wearing his usual black suit jacket, only a long-sleeved black t-shirt and jeans—which still seemed like an odd clothing choice for a hot day.

With his aviator sunglasses, black clothes, and jet-black long hair, Reggie had a signature look and he stuck to it. When I'd first met him, I been a little put off by his appearance. He looked like a hippie vampire.

I'd known Reggie for two years now, and today he didn't wear his usual calm and easygoing expression. His face looked paler than usual, and his lips were pressed tightly together. Maybe it was the pressure of trying to run his business while orchestrating a four-day tournament. Even with my dad's help, the event had to be a huge undertaking.

"How are arrangements for the tournament going?" I asked as he sat down.

"Now that we've got our replacement player, we're set," Reggie said. "The guy was very excited to get the call."

Another reminder for me to talk to my dad—and ask the federal agents how we should handle the situation if it turned out this person had known my dad back in Seattle.

"Can I get you something to drink, Reggie?" Rose asked. "The heat's pretty bad out there."

"I'd love an iced tea latte. With almond milk. Thank you, Rose."

Rose headed for the small fridge behind the counter to get the milk and the pitcher of already-brewed chilled tea.

"We're excited to show you what we've prepared," I

said, as I took a seat across from Reggie. "Beck's just finishing up the chess cake. It's stunning."

"I'd expect nothing less from her." Reggie nodded and smiled.

After Rose brought Reggie a tall clear glass with his tea latte, Beck came in from the back room, pushing a metal cart slowly and carefully. On it was the chess cake, looking breathtakingly perfect and crisp in white chocolate with contrasting chocolate that was so dark it looked black. Chess pieces were perfectly situated on the squares.

"Here it is," Beck said, stopping the cart near the table. She put the brake on the cart's wheels, and as she did it, the cart lurched slightly, and the chocolate king fell on his square.

"No!" Beck looked mortified. "I'm so sorry, Reggie. I thought it was firmly attached."

Reggie looked at the cake, and slowly started to smile. "Don't apologize, Beck. Now it's checkmate. The perfect image for our tournament. In fact, I like it better this way."

Beck's cheeks turned red. "Are you sure? I can fix it on the next cake—the one we bring over Friday."

Reggie shook his head. "I meant what I said. This is perfect. And the way the pieces are lined up, you did have the queen putting the king in check."

Reggie was right. The black queen was set up on a straight diagonal path to the white king.

Beck shrugged and smiled. "I don't know anything about chess. I put the pieces on there to look, well, aesthetically pleasing. I just thought it looked nice."

"Please set it up this way for Friday's cake. It's perfect."

Beck still looked a little puzzled, but she nodded. "Of course, Reggie. I'll make sure it looks just like this."

Beck slid a knife into the cake and cut a slice for Reggie, then put it on a plate and handed him a fork.

Reggie turned the plate toward him. "Look at the black and white checkerboard pattern inside the cake. How do you do these things?" He took a bite and closed his eyes. "Moist and delicious, Beck."

Maeve brought out a plate with the naanini, a bowl of raita, and a napkin—as well as my checkerboard refrigerator cookies.

"I've been looking forward to tasting these sandwiches." Reggie grinned. "Good thing I skipped lunch today."

Since I hadn't had lunch either, I joined in by eating a small slice of cake and one of my cookies, still warm.

Reggie took one half of the naanini and dipped it in the bowl of creamy raita.

"It's nice to have this nod to Indian food, since that's where chess came from," Reggie said, once he'd eaten a few bites of the sandwich. He nodded in approval. "Nice flavor. Very portable way to eat Indian food. If someone wants to take their sandwich out on the balcony or up to their room, it'll be easy."

"We'll have these on the lunch line," I said, "along with two different salads and wraps and our usual sandwiches."

"Perfect," Reggie said. He finished the last of his naanini. "I'd love to have that cake on display in the pedestal case near the lunch station. Everyone will want to see it."

"Beck and I can bring the cake over Friday morning." I turned to her, and she nodded. "Then Daisy, Elise, and I will bring everything else at 10:45 a.m. and get started setting up."

It would be a little crazy, along with our regular busy

Friday morning. Hopefully, with Tyler and Evan working the line at the bakery, we'd be okay.

I took Reggie back to see Biga in his pen and let him hold him for a bit. Biga was so excited, I was afraid he'd pee on him.

Thankfully, he did *not*.

THAT EVENING at 5:45 p.m., after staying later than usual to prep for the next morning, I slid down in my chair to take my first break of the day. I checked my texts and saw that both Tyler and Evan could come in early on Friday to help out. Beck also texted that she wanted to come in early, since she needed to get all her other duties taken care of before she finished the chess cake.

Funny how the mistake of the fallen king piece had ended up making the cake perfect in Reggie's eyes.

The raven I'd seen with Nate last night hadn't been a bad omen.

I hoped the fallen king wasn't one either.

Chapter Four

***Welcome to the 1ˢᵗ Annual River Grove
Chess Tournament***

DAY 1
Friday, August 29

Pairings
Andrew Mehta - Trey Godwin
Younghee Park - Maya Singh
Gunnar Larsen - Patrick Bowman
Kenneth Chen - Aiden McAlister
Rich Haskins - Derek Bartolo

When my alarm rang at 4:00 a.m. that Friday morning, my eyes were already wide open. I was ready to move.

Last night I'd laid out my clothes, slightly fancier than usual since I'd be spending part of the day at the tournament. I wore a green sleeveless blouse and nice, white capri pants with cute, closed-toe sandals—ones that would hold up to me dropping a heavy bag of sugar or flour on them.

I *seemed* wide awake enough, but to make sure, I downed a mug of pre-coffee from my coffeemaker and even ate an egg on toast. I brought out the basket of washed Laughing Loaf aprons and loaded them into the car, then lured Biga into his crate.

Beck parked in the alley behind the bakery just as I pulled up.

"When you said you were coming in early, you meant it," I called out to Beck with a laugh.

She had that focused look in her eye. I knew she was nervous about the cake. Knowing it would be on display all day at The Riverside didn't help with that.

"I want to make this perfect," she said, her tone almost clipped. "I've made family birthday cakes before, but this is my first big cake for the bakery. I don't even know why I'm doing it, Gracie. I'm not experienced enough."

Beck had a perfectionist streak, even though of course, that was part of what made her so good—and The Laughing Loaf benefited from that. I didn't want to console her with "but Reggie loved it," because that would not work. She would still focus in on any detail that was off or not quite right to her, even if it was something no one else would notice.

"You're still coming over with me to transport the cake?"

She nodded. "I'll have everything ready to go. The layers are baked, the frosting's mixed. I just need to assemble, frost, and decorate. I'll put the chess pieces on when we get to The Riverside."

"You may not have the same amount of experience as

other cake bakers, but you have a gift. Your artistic side and baking skills are on point. Can you trust me when I tell you, it's going to be fine?"

I looked at her face, downcast and tense, unlike the usual Beck who greeted me cheerfully every morning.

"I guess so," she said with a sigh.

Beck said she'd be distracted by music this morning, so we went about our duties quietly. I worked on shaping brioche and prepping another batch of naan, while Beck cut up beignets and got them ready for Rose to fry. Then she began filling frittata tins to bake.

By the time Rose and Maeve came in, we were on time with our prep. Rose worked on flatbread for wraps and started a batch of sourdough.

With her more pressing prep chores done, Beck started icing and assembling the cake. She worked quietly at the far counter of the back room, keeping to herself.

By the time we opened at 7:30 a.m., the cake was ready, with the exception of the final placement of the chess pieces.

When I examined it, it looked almost identical to the one she'd made that Reggie had raved about. She took out a carrier and carefully placed the cake in it, while loading a tub with "glue" frosting and putting it in the fridge with the molded chess pieces. She put the cake carrier on the bottom of the industrial fridge to keep it cool. We did have A/C, but with today's hot weather, you couldn't take any chances. We didn't want any sliding layers or melted chess pieces.

"I'm ready, Gracie," she said, taking a deep breath. "We can go over when you get a break."

I wouldn't get a break for a while. Shortly after opening, customers began lining up at the counter. I'd need to work the counter until Maeve was done with her bread prep and could relieve me.

Around 9 a.m., a man came in a backpack slung over his shoulder. He wore clear-framed glasses and his eyes behind them were puffy and red, as if he hadn't slept in a while. He was younger than I was, probably in his early twenties, and had a scruffy head of light brown hair and an academic vibe about him.

"Good morning. What can I get you?" I asked, with a smile.

"I'll take the biggest latte you've got and two beignets," he said, pushing his glasses up on his nose. "I drove here from Seattle overnight. Took me sixteen hours."

Seattle.

I might have jumped just a bit. Could this be the new contender in the chess tournament?

"Then you need at least an extra shot," I said with a smile. "It's on the house. You wouldn't be here for the chess tournament, would you?"

"I'm a last-minute addition. Somebody had to drop out and they asked me." He pushed his glasses back up his nose. "I can't believe I'm finally here."

"You from the university?" I asked, then went to the case to bag two beignets.

"How did you know?" He asked with genuine curiosity. "Just got my masters in physics in June. Heading to Caltech for my doctorate in the fall."

The blood in my veins froze. At that level, this kid would have known of my dad at the very least. He might have been in some of his classes. Did my dad not make the connection when the kid accepted the invitation?

"And what's your name?" I asked with a smile. "So I can know who to cheer for."

Unfortunately, this came out sounding flirtatious, and sure enough, the kid began beaming after I said it. *Yikes.*

"Name's Patrick Bowman." He smiled at me dizzily. "I'll look forward to seeing you at the tournament. Maybe we can have a drink at The Riverside." With a raised eyebrow that he probably thought looked suave and James-Bondesque, he headed to the pickup window to get his latte.

This would be interesting. He'd probably recognize my dad, who was easy to spot. The story when he'd left the university had been that he was retiring and moving away. Would Patrick Bowman ask questions? Should my dad avoid him or just be chill about it?

And the thought that bothered me the most: my father would have chosen this replacement player along with Reggie. He hadn't said anything to me about him.

My dad needed to make a call to the agents about this. I texted him, the frustration rising in me.

> Patrick Bowman just came into the bakery.
>
> Was he one of your students?
>
> You KNEW this and didn't tell me?

In ten minutes, we loaded up the trunk of my car with a first load to take over to the lunch line at The Riverside. Beck gripped the handle of the cake carrier with one hand, her other hand laid protectively across the box of carefully wrapped decorations next to her.

The Riverside was bustling with activity when we got there. Beautiful carved wooden dividers had been set up, separating The Riverside's large, high-ceilinged downstairs into two areas. One was a series of tables, comfy armchairs, and dining chairs pushed into conversational groupings, and at the far side of it, a lunch line had been set up with stacks of plates, silverware receptacles and trays for chilling lunchmeats.

The other side of the room, where the tournament action would happen, featured a row of five small wooden tables, each with two chairs, a board, and a digital move timer. Video cameras on stands were trained on the tables, either for recording the games or displaying them on the screens in the larged fenced-off area for observers, to the left of the tables.

Along the wall to one side of the table hung framed photos of each of the ten competitors, with a paragraph writeup under each. One of the frames was empty; I assumed this was where Patrick Bowman's photo would go. After we set up the chess cake on its stand, I wanted to go back and see who'd be playing and what their backgrounds were.

Reggie met us as we stood waiting.

"Thank you, Beck and Gracie, for being willing to come early. Our chef is bringing out the chilled glass case for the display. He'll be out in just a minute or two."

Beck looked a little shaky. And terrified.

"Let me go look for Jorge," Reggie said, looking toward the door to the kitchen. "I'll be right back."

I pulled Beck aside to one of the conversational groupings. Beck sat the cake carrier onto the table in front of us and we both sat down on the sofa. I studied her face.

"Are you okay, Beck?"

She looked at me with wide, brown eyes. She gulped.

"It's going to be on display all day." Her lower lip trembled. "It's not perfect. I know it's not. Everyone's going to see my mistakes."

I put my hand on hers. "Listen, it doesn't matter if it's not perfect in your eyes. Reggie loves it for how it looks. It says CHESS to everyone who'll see it. That's what they'll see."

This didn't change the look of terror on her face. "Here's some perspective, Beck. There are ten people coming in to play very competitive games of chess. I'm pretty sure most of them feel insecure, like they're going to lose. They're not going to notice mistakes in your cake. They're going to be thinking of their own mistakes."

This seemed to calm Beck down. She opened the cake carrier and looked inside, then closed it.

"Maybe you're right." She turned to me and nodded.

Soon Reggie and Chef Jorge came out from the kitchen, rolling the display case. Reggie plugged the long cord into the wall and lifted the lid.

Beck and I stood up and walked over to the two men.

"Jorge, this is our cakemaker, Beck Rodriguez." Reggie gestured to us. "She created the cake just for the tournament. It's all yours, Beck."

Beck stood up with the carrier and went over to the open case. I held the carrier while she set down the marble pedestal on the stand, then gently lifted the cake out and set it down on it.

"Beck, if you don't need my help, I'm going to ask Reggie a question about the lunch setup."

She turned to me with a look of relief. "I'm good now. Go ahead, Gracie. And thanks."

I went to ask Reggie about a place to store our backup supply of wraps and bread, since there wasn't a lot of storage on the line. When I came back ten minutes later, I gasped as I saw the cake, complete with the chocolate chess board and the fallen king. Beck had lowered the case covering. She stood back, looking at it thoughtfully.

It looked like a display in a museum. Or the centerpiece

of a patisserie window in Paris. The sharp, crisp chess spaces and the shiny white and dark chocolate playing pieces stood out like a work of art. Her chocolate piping around the cake's top and bottom was impeccable.

"What do you think?" I asked her as she stood looking at her creation.

Tears welled up in her eyes as she turned to me. "It looks great. I...I did a good job."
I hugged her. "Let's get back. Now we have work to do at our *other* workplace."

Chapter Five

At 10:30 a.m., Elise and Daisy came in the back door of the Laughing Loaf to pick up the wrapped salad bowls, sandwich fixings, and Maeve's freshly baked flatbread for wraps.

Maeve had just packed the two large, insulated containers with naanini, ready to take over to The Riverside.

With some help from Maeve and me in loading up Elise's car, the two lunch servers drove over to The Riverside to set up the lunch buffet.

Now we could focus on business at The Laughing Loaf.

Thinking of the players coming into town for the tournament, I'd set out an appropriate joke of the day this morning. I thought about all the arrangements the players had to make to get here—flying into San Francisco or San Jose, then renting a car or taking an Uber on the winding road to our tiny town.

Laughing Loaf Joke of the Day
Did you hear about the woman who fainted
on the luggage carousel at the airport?
She was fine. She came round again eventually.

As the day wore on, it was not crazy busy for a Friday. We had a lot of remote workers, sitting at their laptops in t-shirts and shorts, and taking full advantage of the space for most of the morning for the price of an iced latte and a scone. Apart from the occasional noisy business call, they were quiet and busy working.

Beck's anxiety had left her after her cake made its debut. She was now slicing bread for French toast sticks while singing along happily with the loud rock-pop playlist Maeve had put on.

Beck had been coaching Rose on several of her specialties, so she and other bakers could take up the slack and Beck could do more planning and special projects.

Rose had mixed up dough in the food processor and was now fitting it into tart pans, her hair tied up in a bright paisley bandana.

"Beck, the dough on a couple of these is sliding down the sides of the tart pans. What did I do wrong?"

"Touch the dough as little as possible. It's a warm day anyway and your warm hands are going to melt the butter and soften the dough." Beck looked up at the tart pans. "Pop them in the freezer for about ten minutes. They'll harden and you'll be able to get them back into shape."

"Hey, everybody!" Chloe Westerman came in the back door, dressed in a t-shirt from the University of Oregon, which she'd visited with her grandfather a few months ago in preparation for college application season. Her hair was pulled up in a high ponytail to keep her cool. She'd be filling in at the counter and in the back room over the next few days, while we catered the tournament.

"Chloe, I haven't seen you in forever!" Beck called out cheerfully. "How's your summer going?"

Chloe grinned. "It's fun. My job with the rec department is super easy. Just filing and opening mail. Making a few calls to instructors and people who've registered for classes."

"Don't you work with Peony Roberts?" I asked from the oven where I was monitoring the brioche loaves in the last few minutes of baking.

Chloe shook her head and laughed. "Yeah, she's wild. She's trying to get me to take a tai chi class with her through the department. She said she doesn't want to be the youngest. Most people in the class are over eighty."

"Oh, do it." Beck laughed. "I'd love to see you two out in Grove Park on Saturday mornings with the ladies."

Maeve had been working the counter and popped her head in the door of the back room.

"Can anyone take over for me?" She looked around the room. "I've gotta get naan dough mixed."

"I'll do it," Chloe popped up from the stool she was sitting on. "I haven't worked up front since the remodel."

Right after Chloe put her apron on and headed for the counter, Tyler and Evan came in the back door for their lunch shift, dressed in light t-shirts and shorts.

"Gracie, it's okay to wear shorts, isn't it?" Tyler asked, pulling his red, curly hair up into what looked like a man bun.

"As long as they're not cutoff—" I looked over at him and realized he was indeed wearing cutoffs, the hillbilly kind. I snorted. "I guess it won't be that bad with your apron on."

Tyler smirked. "I promise I'll wear my formal shorts next time."

Evan nodded and took an apron from the clean basket. "I'm wearing my dad's cargo shorts. *I* got the memo."

Tyler snickered. "Those are sweet, bruh."

Aproned and ready, they went to the industrial fridge and pulled out the lunch meats, produce, and salad fixings and went in to set up for lunch.

I heard Chloe greet them and all three were soon laughing.

"Hey, Beck, I'd like to go back to The Riverside after we close, just to check in with Reggie and see how lunch went."

Beck looked up from the bread she was slicing. "That should be fine. We'll all be working on our usual prep. Maeve has to leave for Napa earlier today—so she'll be gone by 4:00 p.m."

Our assistant bread baker left on Fridays to drive up to Napa, since she had a weekend job at a bakery there. To fill in for her, Rose came in for half days on the weekend. Rose was getting the advantage of that weekend time to learn her baking craft from Beck and me in a less stressful atmosphere.

So far, splitting our staff between the bakery and The Riverside was working out okay. I'd touch base with Reggie and find out more soon.

I hadn't heard back from my dad after my angry text.

I wondered if he'd met up with Patrick Bowman in person yet.

THE HARDEST PART of working in an air-conditioned workplace is when you leave it to go out into 89 degree weather.

It's kind of a shock.

Which would be worse—getting into a car that had been sitting in the sun all day and driving over? Or walking four blocks in the heat, just dealing with it till I was acclimated?

I walked. After taking Biga out for a quick walk in the alley, I put him in his pen with some food and new water and left for the tournament.

In the past five hours, The Riverside had transformed into a busy, noisy hub. The entry area was filled with players, their suitcases, and for some of them, their partners. People unfamiliar to me sat in chairs in the lobby, waiting to check in. Reggie's manager of housekeeping, Willow Barrett, was making the rounds of the guests, handing out keys. The Riverside was a big old house that Reggie had remodeled from a commune from his hippie days in 1970s River Grove. I'm not sure they were the original keys, but they definitely looked old.

Others had made their way over to the lunch area, and even after the lunch line had closed down, they sat at tables and couches chatting. Plates of pastries sat on the tables. I grabbed a napkin and took a round flaky one with me.

This would be my lunch.

A small group stood in front of the glass case displaying Beck's chess cake. I took out my phone, moved a little closer and snapped a photo of it to show Beck.

The odd thing about this—seeing as it was taking place in laidback River Grove—was how formal the chess players looked as they gathered at The Riverside. Despite the hot weather, no one wore shorts, with the exception of a couple of women who looked like they could be wives of players. None of the players even wore jeans.

Two players sat at one of the chess tables near the bar,

drinking beer and playing what looked like a fierce game, moving pieces around in a flurry of taps and clicks. It looked incredibly fast compared to the super-slow, overthought moves I made in my games with my dad.

The Riverside had just enough guest rooms for everybody in the tournament. From now through Labor Day, it was going to be a full house.

As I walked in, I looked around the large room and saw Drake, who happened to be working at the bar. Last fall, Drake had helped me hide when two Russian spies tracked me and my friend Elana down in The Riverside.

"Drake, is Reggie around?"

He smiled as he wiped down the bar. "He's upstairs, trying to make arrangements for an offsite dinner for one of the players—it's the guy's anniversary today. Hold on, Gracie. I'll let him know you're here."

My dad had to be here somewhere. I scanned the room. He wasn't in the lunch/mingling area. Or around the chess tables.

Then I looked over at the area in front of the large stone hearth, which wasn't going to be used for a fire anytime soon.

My dad was sitting in a chair in front of the hearth, talking excitedly with Patrick Bowman.

I groaned. Which should I deal with first: check in with Reggie on how catering was going? Or try to figure out if my dad had blown our witness protection cover?

Reggie came down the stairs from his upstairs office. He nodded at me and met me at the bar. His face looked paler today and his movements looked slower. I blamed it on the source of everything bad today: the nearly 90 degree temperatures.

"Want a cold beer?" he asked.

I had a lot more work to do back at the bakery. "No, thanks. Sparkling water sounds good, though."

Drake poured lemon Pellegrino into a glass of ice and handed it to me.

"How did it go today?" I asked Reggie, a little nervous, since this was our biggest catering gig yet.

"It went well. Let's go sit down."

I followed Reggie to a couple of seats near the bar, which overlooked the river. He looked distant and a little preoccupied. Which made sense, since today was the first day of the event he'd been planning for months.

"Daisy and Elise did a great job—kept up a nice chatter with the players," Reggie said, tapping nervously on the arm of the chair. "They kept the line moving. Players and their guests said the food was delicious. We do have too much salad left over, since the sandwiches and wraps were the most popular items. So send a lot less tomorrow. The naan sandwich is a keeper, though. We heard lots of compliments."

"That's good to hear." I blew out a sigh. I'd heard something in Reggie's voice. I waited for him to tell me that something hadn't worked so well. "Okay, I'm waiting for the 'but.'"

Reggie shook his head. "Gracie, everything went great today. It's not a *but*. It's an 'and.'"

I gave him a puzzled look.

"I wanted to ask if Beck would be up for creating another cake for tomorrow. People are coming over to the case just to stare at it. They ate all your checkerboard cookies, but they're gathering and carrying on conversations around her cake. It's a work of art."

I nodded. "Beck's an artist. And when she was

designing and making this cake, she was a *tortured* artist. She wanted it to be perfect."

"I'm used to working with creatives." Reggie nodded sympathetically. "This is last minute, and if she can't fit it in, don't even worry about it. I just thought I'd ask."

I frowned as I considered this. This was a question for me only because the cake had been part of our catering order for the tournament. If he'd be working with Beck directly, she could make this decision. If she felt anxious again about this cake like she did with the first, she had to decide if it was worth it to her.

"Reggie, why don't you ask her? It should be her call."

I texted him Beck's cell phone number.

"Good idea, Gracie." He nodded. "I'll get in touch with her."

After that, Reggie and I chatted for a few minutes about the tournament.

"It's been a treat to work with your dad on this. His enthusiasm has brought back my love for chess. I'm grateful for that." There was a deep sadness in his face, and I wasn't sure where it was coming from. "He's studied each player's moves. He knows their style, their record in previous tournaments. He's got his favorites."

None of this surprised me. My dad had been looking forward to this tournament since Reggie had proposed the idea not long after the two began bonding over chess last year.

Reggie leaned against the bar and smiled, his eyes hidden by his usual mirrored aviator sunglasses. "It's been a lot of work, but it's going well. We've got some amazing players here, and I can't wait to watch them play."

He leaned in toward me and gestured to a very young woman with large brown eyes who'd just walked into the main room, heading for the lunch line. She nervously looked around at the other players in the dining area. A heavyset woman wearing a pink sari followed closely behind her.

"The young woman over there is Maya Singh, here with her mother. She's just turned eighteen. She won a regional tournament recently. She's our closest player—from nearby Saratoga."

He gestured toward a man wearing a blazer and khaki slacks, who was heading for a table with a croissant and coffee. "This is one of our stars, Andrew Mehta. The highest ranked player here. He's from San Diego. Just graduated from University of California there. One of the best players in US chess and he's only twenty-two."

The young man was good-looking and wore a mysterious smile on his face. A look which was probably intimidating if you were sitting across from him in a chess match.

"He's expected to win here?" I asked Reggie.

He shrugged and smiled faintly.

"There's only one player here close to his ranking. Each player will play others with a similar ranking. But players with the highest rankings don't always win."

"So there may be some surprises?" I asked, still watching the young man as he found a seat and sat down by himself.

"They're always fun." Reggie smiled. "Who wants predictability anyway?"

I took a sip of my drip coffee. "My dad. He lives for it." My father and Patrick Bowman had just gotten up from their spot by the hearth. My dad gave me a wave and smiled.

"That's why it's good that your dad and I are both

running this," Reggie said, looking down at his phone and frowning at something. "We balance each other out."

I finished off my pastry. It was a *kouign-amann*, and I wished another one would materialize on my plate. My mouth was crying out for more of the buttery, caramelized crunchiness.

"My father taught me about chess's roots in India when I was growing up. A game called *chaturanga*." Reggie nodded at the name. "Even back then," I said, "it was all about bringing the king down."

Reggie smiled. He put his hand on my arm and pointed at a group of players walking past us, carrying plates filled with pastry.

"If you're interested, here come some of the other players."

I turned to watch the group as they took seats in the chairs in front of the stone fireplace on the other side of the bar.

"That young woman with her hair in a bun—that's Younghee Park from Orange County. Brilliant player. She's been playing since she was three."

The young woman looked quiet and reserved. While her companions laughed, she took a sip of coffee and smiled softly. Reggie watched her for a moment. "I don't think she realizes how good she is. Out of anyone in the group, she's got the best chance to beat Andrew Mehta."

"On her left is Derek Bartolo. He's the oldest of the players—in his fifties. He's good but has a reputation as a poor loser. He likes to claim his situation was unfair. Or that his opponent broke the rules."

Reggie studied the three competitors as they ate their pastry. The thin young man in the chair nearest us had white-blonde, buzz-cut hair and wore horn-rimmed glasses.

"This guy is Trey Godwin. He wants to be *known* as a chess champion more than any real love he has for the game. He works harder at it than anyone else here. When he loses, it's because he's prepared the same moves as everyone else and memorized them. Unfortunately, most players see him coming."

I tried to imagine the five tables that would be filled with competitors soon. People who loved chess and probably thought about it even more than Nate thought about birds. These players were probably even more competitive and chess-obsessed than my dad if that was even possible.

Games would continue today, tomorrow, and Sunday. Monday morning, Labor Day, the official tournament would end with a final round, and the floor would be set up for the informal community competition. That time was open to unranked players from River Grove, the coast, and Silicon Valley, anyone local who wanted to come in to be paired for games.

Nate would be here. And I'm sure he'd be happy to play *anyone* other than his usual opponent, my dad.

Chapter Six

I did have to get back to the bakery, but I wanted to find my dad first.

I went downstairs and looked for him by the chairs at the fireplace where he was before, but he wasn't there.

Soon I heard a familiar Surrey accent coming from the conversation area in the dining side of the hall. My father was sitting on a sofa across from the young man with smooth brown skin—Andrew Mehta. I moved in their direction, passing by Beck's cake on display.

Andrew was gesturing with his hands as he explained something about moving a bishop. My father nodded, then leaned forward, his fingers steepled, as he listened to the young man.

Andrew's phone buzzed on the table in front of them. He picked it up, frowning at the screen.

"Excuse me, John," Mehta said distractedly. "I've got to take this call. It's been good to meet you."

With that, the man got up and left in a hurry out the front doors of The Riverside.

Now was my chance, before anyone else grabbed his attention.

"Dad," I said as I sat down on the sofa across from him.

"What is it, dear?" He turned to me with a euphoric smile. He was ensconced in his happy place at this event. Maybe as he lived out this dream, keeping his former identity a secret had slipped to a lower priority in his mind.

"Earlier I saw you talking to Patrick Bowman, that new player *from Seattle*." I took a deep breath and tried to be calm. I kept my voice to a whisper. It was hard to chide him; he was bubbling over with joy, oblivious to any possible wrongdoing on his part. "Did he recognize you? As far as your old students and colleagues are concerned, you retired and moved out of the Seattle area. You are not Dr. Jonathan Hollis anymore." I pulled the tournament program from my pocket. "You're listed as Dr. John Markley here."

A cloud passed over his face. He looked down at his lap. "He did recognize me. He called me Dr. Hollis. And yes, I did talk to him, Gracie. For quite a while. He's done well for himself, and I'm proud of him."

"You knew his name before he got here. You *knew* he was your former student."

"Oh dear," he said, a downcast look on his face. "I was excited to see he was coming to the tournament, and I wasn't sure he'd remember me from the university."

I groaned. "But wasn't he your student? Did you tell him your new name or that you were living here?"

He shook his head. "He *was* my student. But it didn't come up. We only talked about the tournament—and some international chess news that had caused quite a stir recently—the reigning world chess champion was ejected from a game because he wore jeans. Complete violation of the dress code and quite a shocker. That's all."

I thought about it. There might be a way out of this.

"Dad, please talk to the agents and let them know. See what they say. Will you?"

My father nodded. "I've got my burner phone with me. I'll go up to Reggie's conference room upstairs and contact them now. People are still checking in, and I've got time before our first round at four."

I sighed with relief. Then hugged him. "Please do. Thank you."

The air was a little cooler as I walked back to The Laughing Loaf. I hoped my dad called the agents. It was possible that if we didn't make a big deal out of it, Patrick would think my dad had come to the tournament from wherever he'd gone to retire. It would call attention to this situation to use his new name. Maybe Patrick hadn't noticed the name on the program. Our federal agents, Maura and Jeremy, might think it best to let things go.

Maeve had left for her weekend job up in Napa, but everyone else was hard at work in the Laughing Loaf back room when I came back in. Chloe was chopping herbs for the frittatas Beck was making. She and Rose (who was now mixing beignet dough) were exchanging info about their favorite local thrift shops.

Beck had started up a mixer, whipping what looked like buttercream frosting.

I assumed Reggie had called her.

"Your cake is the biggest attraction at the tournament right now. Look at this." I scrolled through my photos for the picture of chess players standing in front of her cake in the display case.

She smiled softly as she looked at the photo. "Reggie called and asked if I could do a cake for tomorrow night."

"Well, you're making frosting, so I guess you said yes."

She nodded. "It'll be some work—and most of it I'll be working on at home."

"Beck, this is your job. This is not for The Laughing Loaf. You get to decide what to charge. And make sure you count all the time you put in. Reggie knows it's a rush job."

She frowned. "But that will be a lot of money then. I feel weird asking for that much."

"Reggie understands you have to pay for quality. He really likes your work."

"If it's not for the bakery, I shouldn't be working on it here," she said, hesitating.

"If you've got time today after taking care of everything else, I have no problem with you working on the cake. As long as we can finish everything we need for Saturday."

Beck had told me last month that she was worried that if she had a child—which she and Sam were hoping to do soon —she'd have to give up her job at the bakery.

Custom cake baking was something she could do at home if she needed to. She could get a cottage business license from the county and take the required food safety class. It would be helpful for her to get a taste of running her own business. How to calculate prices so she made a profit, how to multitask, even how to network and to get the word out about her business.

"Just to check—you're good with making the cake for Reggie?" I asked. "And you *want* to do this?"

She nodded enthusiastically. "This is a good test of how well I can work on my own." She looked at me, assessing my reaction. "You know, in case I wanted to do that on the side someday."

So Beck had been considering the possibility herself.

"I can't wait to see what this next one looks like." I grinned.

Beck and I did a quick run through of what needed to be done before we left. Beck had Chloe start the cinnamon roll dough, since it was something the young woman had done many times before. But without Maeve, I was the sole bread maker. There was a lot to bake for tomorrow with the regular Saturday lunch service and catering for The Riverside.

Before I plunged into that, I took Biga out for a walk in the alley. When I came into his room, he gave me a pitiful, passive-aggressive look: *Oh, so* now *you want to spend time with me?*

We walked up and down the alley, and Biga put his mark on many plants and telephone poles—some of which looked like they'd been visited a little too often by the local dog community.

After that, I deposited Biga in his pen, washed my hands thoroughly, and sat down in a chair next to the industrial mixer, trying to get a double batch of flatbread dough mixed.

If we regularly ran out of flatbread on the lunch line at the bakery, we'd probably run out of it at The Riverside.

I LEFT at 4:30 p.m., leaving Beck to work on her cake for Reggie. She seemed to have more confidence on this one; I didn't see signs of the obsessive perfectionism she'd shown with the first chess cake. She'd drawn a sketch of what she wanted the final to look like. I saw a glimpse of it and noticed it featured a ring of redwood trees, which I assumed she'd mold from chocolate. This looked more ambitious than her first cake.

I couldn't wait to see it tomorrow. I hoped Beck would get some sleep tonight.

I got into my car, with Biga in the back in his crate.

On my way home, I heard my burner phone buzz in my purse. The agents.

I pulled into the carport at home, turned off the car, and went to listen to the message. It was agent Jeremy LaValle.

"Good evening, Gracie. Your dad called about running into a former student at the chess match. He admitted he slipped up and responded to his old name. I'm not too worried--*yet*. This may not be as bad as it seems."

I'd wait to talk to my dad inside before I called Jeremy back. I took Biga's crate out and unlocked the front door. I opened the door to him standing there, looking excited.

"Gracie, did you get my text? I wanted to know if you'd join me in watching a match."

I thought I'd heard my phone vibrate in my purse right before I locked up at the bakery. I hadn't gotten a chance to check it.

"I'd wanted to watch Park and Mehta's game, but the timing won't work for me," I said, as I closed the door and let Biga out of his crate. "Who's playing?"

"It's Patrick Bowman and Kenneth Chen."

"Sure. I'd love to see a game."

"Then Reggie asked if you could join us for the group dinner. Nate's welcome, too. They've got extra spots since one of the players, Gunnar Larsen, is going out for an anniversary dinner with his wife. Would you be up for it? Chef Jorge is making steak—with *haricots verts* and roasted cauliflower."

The steak had more appeal for my dad, but I would happily eat anything Reggie's chef made.

"Nate's at his shoot in Monterey tonight, so he can't come." I stooped down and picked up Biga, who was looking up at me eagerly. "I'm sure this guy would love to get his paws on some of that steak. Is there any place at The Riverside we can set up for him?"

"Reggie said he can stay in the utility room near the kitchen. He'll set it up for him like he did last Christmas."

There were many reasons why I was happy to ditch making dinner at home tonight. I'd get food way better than anything I could make; Chef Jorge was brilliant. And I'd get to meet the tournament players and chat.

"Sounds great." Then I remembered about my dad's slip up with Patrick Bowman today. "By the way, I got a text from Jeremy. I think we should do a call with him later, after we eat."

A relaxed smile settled into place on my father's face. "No need to, dear. He called me back and said it should be okay. I responded to the Dr. Hollis name and simply acted as if everything was normal. Jeremy said I should continue with that."

I was skeptical of this advice.

I picked up Biga's tote bag and filled it with his bowl and some toys.

"Dad, remember--your name's on the program as Dr. John Markley."

My dad held up his hands. "I'm not going to bring it up," he said matter-of-factly. "I will respond when someone calls me John, which should suffice."

I gave him a doubtful look as I set down Biga's carrier and lured him in. I passed my boy a treat through the grate.

"Maybe Jeremy's plan to not make a big deal out of it will be fine. It still makes me feel uncomfortable."

My dad looked a little embarrassed and also like he really wanted to change the subject. Which he did.

I carried the crate out to my car, while my dad grabbed the tote.

"That Andrew Mehta is such an interesting player. What a mind he has. I did ask him if he'd play a game with me, but he got an urgent call and had to leave."

"Maybe he'll have more time on Monday after his games are over."

"Possibly," my dad said, still looking disappointed as he got into the passenger seat.

"I think you'll enjoy this evening, Gracie. Reggie's got a band playing and the bar is open, of course. I wanted to play chess, but most of the players are sitting it out. Playing as many games as they do, it's exhausting."

"Hey, Reggie told me a little bit about the games over the weekend, but I'm curious," I said. "How do they decide who's won the tournament?"

"The players will be scored for their wins throughout the rounds over the weekend, and the tournament winner will be the one with the most points at the end."

"I think Reggie told me about this. I always thought chess tournaments were elimination tournaments. Like basketball."

My dad shook his head. "That would be a knockout tournament, dear. Not common for chess. We wanted to have all the players engaged in matches through Monday."

As my father went on to talk about the different types of chess tournaments, my mind started to wander.

It would be fun to go over to The Riverside, to hear the

band, eat a really good dinner, and have a few drinks. For a moment, I thought about inviting my best friend and partner-in-cocktails, Elana Schiffer. But while Reggie would definitely make an exception for Nate and me, he might not for Elana. My friend, though I loved her, did not have much interest in chess.

And a bored Elana was not a fun Elana.

WE ARRIVED at 5:15 p.m., just in time for the game. The Riverside's downstairs was pretty quiet. Maybe players were upstairs getting ready for dinner.

After getting a couple of Pimm's cups from Drake to take the edge off a long hot day, I slid into the seat next to my dad in the *skittles* area—the area set aside for watching games and often playing informal, pickup games.

There were a few other players in this section: Aiden McAlister and Rich Haskins, who sat at a table with a chess board. I wondered if the game they were watching got boring, they'd play their own.

With no mom in sight, Maya Singh sat cross-legged with her shoes off in a comfy chair in front of us, eating checkerboard cookies and guzzling soda. She'd brought a school composition book with her to take notes.

"What's your prediction, Dad?" I handed him his drink.

"This could go either way," he said, tilting his head. "I'm inclined to say Patrick will win, but that could be because I know him better. I know he'll be the one taking chances."

The two sat down at the table to wait for the game time. Patrick was playing white pieces, so he went first. He quickly moved up a pawn and tapped the timer, which was on Kenneth's right.

Kenneth responded by moving his pawn to a position next to Patrick's.

After about ten minutes of play, I whispered to my dad. "They seem to be making such safe moves."

"True—but oh, hold on a minute." My dad peered over at the board. "Look at that. Patrick's set up a *fork*—his knight has Kenneth's king in check in one direction and he can take his bishop in the other. Well done."

Kenneth stared at the board with a look of fierce concentration, as if he could will his pieces to move themselves out of danger.

"Can Kenneth survive this?" I whispered to my dad. It didn't look like he had many options.

My dad looked over at the video screen, which displayed a close-up view of the gameplay.

"He could move his king, but that would be delaying the inevitable. Patrick could check him on the other side by moving up his pawn."

Our eyes were riveted on the screen to see what would happen next.

Kenneth stared down at the board and let out a sigh. Then he knocked his king over, signifying he knew the game was over.

As we looked at the table to see what would happen next, Kenneth reached across the board to shake Patrick's hand. With a smile, Kenneth took his play book and red pencil, got up and headed toward the stairs. Patrick looked down at the board, a big grin spreading across his face.

After the game, the skittles area cleared out as players got ready for dinner.

On the small, raised stage, a trio set up and then played: a drummer, a bass player, and a keyboard-playing female vocalist wearing a red and blue catsuit who looked like she'd decided on a superhero look.

While my father went to look for Reggie, I strolled by

the bar, looking at the player photos posted on the wall. Patrick Bowman's photo was now up—it featured him staring down over a chess board, his hand poised above a piece.

I noticed Younghee Park and young Maya Singh were the only women among the ten players on the wall.

Since Younghee had been playing since childhood, maybe she had gotten used to being one of the few women at a competition. I could relate to that, having often been one of a small group of women in my computer science classes in college. I'd get excited when there were other women in my class, but the lack of them bothered me less and less the more classes I took. I liked the subject, and being in the minority didn't discourage me from studying it.

I looked over at the players by the bar, all of them engaged in conversation. Younghee was smiling, listening sympathetically to Trey Godwin, the thin, pale young man she'd been sitting in front of the fireplace with today. I'd heard someone mention that Trey had lost to Andrew Mehta in today's round. I was interested in talking to Younghee and curious to hear how Trey was feeling about his game with Mehta.

"Hey, you're the bakery lady," said Patrick Bowman, who looked like he was riding high after his win. "You're name's Gracie, right?"

"Ready for your next rounds?" I asked with a polite smile, looking past him to Younghee and pretty much anyone else in the room but him.

"Uh, yeah. I just *won*." He narrowed his eyes and smiled. "I've been refining my strategy, and I'm ready to take Mehta down tomorrow."

"Why are you so sure you'll beat him?" I asked. "From what I've read, he's pretty tough to beat."

A flash of anger crossed his face, then passed, as his lips curled up into a smile. "Oh, I have a plan that he's not going to be prepared for. Just wait and see." He gave me a onceover, head-to-toe, and lowered his voice. He jammed his hands into his pants pockets like a fifteen-year-old. "Hey, this band's really great. Up for a dance before dinner?"

"No thanks, Patrick. I need to talk about a catering issue with Reggie." I took a deep breath and looked around to see if I could locate the saloon owner. "Good luck on your matches tomorrow."

I felt obligated to touch base with Reggie, since I'd used him as my excuse. I saw him over by the lunch line, near Andrew Mehta.

Oblivious to Patrick's scheming, Mehta stood over by Beck's cake on display, surrounded by a large group of players laughing and chatting.

"What player here are you most afraid of, Mehta?" One of the younger players asked the champion. I'd seen his face on the wall of photos—Aiden McSomething.

Mehta thought about it and took a sip from his drink. "It has to be Younghee Park. She's an outstanding player."

A few of the guys around Mehta laughed, and one of them whistled. They threw out a few cracks about her looks —which made me mad. It bothered me that Mehta seemed to be laughing, too.

I made my way over to Reggie and pulled him aside.

"Reggie, I'm using you as an excuse to get away from someone. So I'm asking you if there's anything else you might need for the lunch tomorrow—maybe more chess-board cookies to put out for snacks during the day?"

Reggie snickered and glanced over to where Patrick wandered listlessly near the dance floor. "Feel free to use me as an excuse. If you wanted to bring more cookies, they would definitely get eaten."

"Thanks, Reggie. How are things going for you on this first day?"

He shrugged. "No issues. The round today went well. I'm enjoying being around the players. So far the competition is friendly and fierce, if that makes sense."

I frowned, thinking of Patrick's comments about taking Mehta down. "I hope it stays that way."

A few minutes later, the band wrapped up their set and Reggie walked onto the stage to announce dinner.

My father and I made our way toward the head of the table where Reggie would sit.

After we were seated, Younghee pulled out the chair next to me. Aiden—who I now realized was Aiden McAlister, was still a college student. He took a seat on the other side of Younghee.

Younghee turned to me, an eager look on her pretty, porcelain-smooth face.

"So you're the caterer. Gracie, right? I heard you run a bakery downtown. Everyone says it's really good. I'm a big fan of sweets."

"My bakery's been serving lunch here. If you like sweets, we have a lot. Come check us out tomorrow."

"Perfect," she said with a smile, pulling her napkin out and spreading it on her lap, as a waiter set salad plates down in front of us. "My match isn't till later tomorrow, so I'll have some time."

Aiden launched into a discussion of who at the tournament he'd met previously—only Andrew Mehta and Trey Godwin, since both had come to a tournament in his college town. Younghee had been in matches with both, so they leaned over the table, excitedly comparing playing styles and past games.

I couldn't keep up with the conversation with my minimal chess knowledge, but my dad jumped in to comment and soon they were immersed in the details of *skewering* and *forking*—the move Patrick had used on Kenneth. Feeling like an outsider, I grabbed my phone to check my texts.

After we'd eaten the steak, I sat back and poured a half glass of the cabernet the kitchen staff had set out for dinner. Younghee did the same. I turned to her.

"So what's it like being a woman at a chess tournament like this?"

"Yeah." Younghee rolled her eyes and let out a long sigh. "It can be lonely. But I grew up with it. I never seemed to connect with the few women I met at tournaments. There's a few more female players now, but you'd think there'd be more."

I nodded. "I was a computer science major in school. I know what you mean."

"No way," Younghee said excitedly. "I was a comp sci major. I'm a software engineer."

"You like it?" I asked.

"I like chess better," she said, shrugging. "But I'm not good enough to make a living at it. Writing software works for me."

I told her a quick, edited version of my move away from the tech industry—without any mention of witness protection or my ex-husband.

"I always loved baking," I told her. "I wanted to do something where I could make something *real*—not like code or some business software. I wanted to sink my hands into dough. I wanted to see the looks on people's faces when they tasted what I baked. Baked goods are a great way to make people happy."

"I totally agree with that." Younghee smiled. "Now I *know* I have to come to your bakery tomorrow."

We talked for a while. I saw Andrew Mehta at the opposite end of the table. He was surrounded by players who leaned in, listening to him intently as if he were going to dispense deep words of chess wisdom. Lights above reflected on a fine sheen of sweat on his face, which seemed odd since the room was air-conditioned and felt like a comfortable temperature.

I noticed Younghee casting quick glances down the table at Mehta. I understood that—he was a striking man, with high cheekbones, smooth skin, and a physique that looked like he probably worked out when he wasn't in front of a chess board. But as she kept surreptitiously glancing in his direction, I wondered if there was something more between them.

My dad and I chatted with players and their partners till almost eight fifteen, when I could no longer control my yawning. I nudged my dad, and he nodded.

He turned to Reggie, who'd just finished a piece of Beck's fallen king cake.

"We should get Biga and then get going, Reggie. It'll be an early morning for both of us."

"Good meeting you tonight, Younghee," I smiled at the young woman I'd bonded with tonight.

"Same here, Gracie! I'll see you tomorrow morning at the bakery."

As SOON AS we got home, I flopped onto my bed, followed by Biga, who was very eager for my attention. I cuddled with him and hid his squeaky toy in the covers, then laughed as he nosed around, completely clueless, trying to find it.

At 9:00 p.m., Nate called from his hotel in Monterey. Since I could reveal aspects of my witness protection life to him now, I told him about my dad possibly blowing our cover with one of his former students.

"Why am I not surprised?" He said softly. "He's distracted because he's having so much fun. He's been looking forward to this for months. He was excited to see a former student."

"Yeah. Still, he isn't on his guard. And that worries me. Even though the agents say the best thing to do now is nothing. Just let it go."

I also worried about what Patrick would do if he figured out my dad was listed as a different name. There was something about the kid from Seattle that I didn't trust. He made me nervous.

"Maybe you should take the agent's word for it, Gracie," Nate said, his voice deep and throaty. "Don't go looking for things to worry about."

I told him about Beck and her nervousness about the chess cake.

"That was a great idea to let her deal with the new cake with Reggie. This might help her. She doesn't have to worry about pleasing you—just Reggie, her customer."

I frowned. "You think Beck is worried about letting me down?" I hadn't thought of that.

"She adores you. You asked her to create this cake and she worried she didn't have enough experience to make a cake good enough to represent The Laughing Loaf. Now she just has to please one person. And it's her reputation on the line, not The Laughing Loaf's."

I'd never thought about it that way. I felt in my gut that this was a good opportunity for Beck, but I wasn't fully sure why.

For my assistant manager, and where she was in her life, this project could be the start of a new and more flexible part-time job.

The downside of it was, I might eventually lose my brilliant pastry whiz to her own business.

Chapter Seven

DAY 2
River Grove Chess Tournament
Saturday, August 30

Pairings
Trey Godwin - Derek Bartolo
Aiden McAlister – Kenneth Chen
Patrick Bowman – Rich Haskins
Maya Singh - Gunnar Larsen
Andrew Mehta - Younghee Park

On Saturdays, the bakery opened a little later than on weekdays.

I got time to sleep in.

The most wonderful feeling in the world is when you wake up, look at your alarm, and realize you can sleep in longer.

I lay back in the bed and dozed blissfully for a half an hour and then sprung out of the bed. Saturday was family day. I loved the relaxed, friendly atmosphere at the bakery.

And today the tournament revved up, with new pairings of players. I wanted to be there for at least part of the time. I was looking forward to meeting the brilliant Andrew Mehta.

And I'd get to see Beck's second chess cake on display.

At 6:00 a.m., I saw Beck in the alley, carrying a large box and a canvas bag stuffed to the brim.

As I heard her come up the back steps, I rushed to the door and held it open.

"Need any help?"

Beck smiled. "No, I'm good. Sam is bringing the rest."

Soon Sam, looking sleepy-eyed, approached the steps carrying another box.

"Good morning, Sam!" I called to him, continuing to hold the door. "Can I make you some coffee? You probably don't get up at this hour on weekends."

Sam Rodriguez was a cabinet maker, who went to job sites all over Silicon Valley bright and early during the week.

"No, thanks, Gracie." Sam stifled a yawn. "I'm going home after this and getting back in bed. I'm not cut out for bakers' hours."

He came in and set the box down at Beck's work station. I could see an impressive assortment of fondant packs, bags of powdered sugar, piping bags, and tools.

"I got most of my prep done yesterday, so I think I'll have time to finish the cake this morning. Reggie said as long as I brought it over to The Riverside by 3:00 p.m., it was fine."

"After we close, I can help you take it over," I said, excited to see what Beck had come up with. "Is there more involved this time?"

Beck nodded and yawned. "It was a lot more work. I went to bed at 4:00 a.m."

What could I say? I'd stayed up all night to finish jobs when I worked in tech. You do what you have to do. Beck had been given a very short deadline.

I dumped the flatbread dough out on the floured tabletop and put the mixing bowl back on the machine.

"Are you still glad you took on the job?"

Beck smiled. "I had so much fun with this design. I feel good about it. Of course, maybe I'm just loopy from not getting much sleep."

Sam looked at me. "No really, it's incredible. Better than the first one. Wait till you see it, Gracie."

"I'm excited now." I looked over at Sam. "No coffee, but would you like a scone? They're blueberry white chocolate. I just took them out of the oven."

"The only right answer to that is *yes*," he said, grinning.

I picked two scones off the baking rack and laid them into a clam shell container.

"Thanks!" Sam said gratefully as I handed it to him. "I'll eat one and then go back to bed."

After planting a kiss on Beck's cheek, he went out the back door.

I hadn't put on a playlist yet.

"Are you okay with music today?"

Beck nodded. "Music sounds great. Something upbeat. Seriously, I need it to keep me awake."

I put on a playlist of pop with familiar songs we could all sing along to.

I separated the flatbread dough into balls, then flattened them and laid them out in pans, ready to bake after they had a short rise. We would make full use of the many racks of our combi oven today, between flatbread and naan. Good thing we had enough brioche for the bakery and The Riverside.

At seven, Rose and Chloe came in and got to work. Rose could now take on the entire beignet process, freeing Beck to work on her cake. Chloe set to work putting together pans of cinnamon rolls, from the dough she'd mixed yesterday. She also baked the trays of scones I had in the freezer, then started filling tarts.

It was going to be another busy morning, but the staff was great. We'd get through it.

I was at the counter when we opened, so I got to welcome people coming in—one of my favorite duties at the bakery. I loved the families who came in on the weekend—kids in strollers or toddling beside their parents. I always found some small treat to give the young children.

Today, I recognized a few of the players from the chess tournament in line.

A little after eight, I saw my new friend Younghee in line, eyeing the display case from afar.

"Good morning, Younghee. You sure didn't waste any time getting over here."

The woman laughed. "I am *very* motivated by treats."

"Me and my dog, too," I said, laughing. "What sounds good? We've got tarts, cinnamon rolls, muffins, and scones."

Younghee brightened as she went over to look at the case. "Oh wow, that strawberry tart right there. I'd love to get that to go, with a large latte made with 2 percent milk."

"You got it. How are you feeling about your matches?"

She sighed. "Well, it will be interesting. I'm playing my ex-boyfriend. Final game of the day. Hoping I can stay focused."

Being a snoop, I was curious. "Who's your ex?"

"Andrew Mehta. Drew and I broke up last year. Or

rather, he broke up with me." She shook her head and laughed but it was definitely a bitter laugh. "TMI here. I don't know why I'm telling you. I guess—well, I'm kind of hoping it doesn't get weird."

I nodded. This explained the glances she'd given him last night.

"I hope it doesn't either. Should I hope he loses?" I flashed her a conspiratorial smile.

She snorted as she ran her credit card through the pay station. "Not much chance of that. He is Andrew Mehta, after all. Everyone who plays chess wants to *be* him. And he knows it."

I handed her one of our pink boxes with a strawberry tart in it.

"Then I hope he messes up big time, Younghee."

She giggled and gave me a thumbs up. "Thanks, Gracie," she whispered.

Not longer after, Patrick Bowman stood in front of me, grinning with bedhead hair and his glasses slightly askew. "Gracie, I'd like a latte with whole milk. And give me one of those big cinnamon rolls."

"Got it," I said with a friendly smile. "How are you feeling about your matches today, Patrick?"

"You saw my win yesterday. I'm playing Mehta tomorrow, and I've studied all his openings. I am pretty sure—" he looked at me and lowered his voice as he leaned across the counter. "—I'll beat him to a pulp."

I gave him a cheerful smile. Whoa. This guy had no lack of confidence.

"The guy has a system, Gracie." He tapped his head. "If you look at this past year—in the games he's played—he's predictable. When he changes his moves, I know exactly what he's going to do. I actually wrote a software program that figures it out."

I'd have to ask my dad about this, since my dad had also tried to figure out Mehta's system.

"There was a reason I got called to play in this tournament," Bowman said, his eyes narrowing. "It's fate. This year I'm going to win it. Mehta will see for the first time how it feels to lose."

Hoping my face didn't show my skepticism, I handed him his cinnamon roll in a clam shell.

"By the way, Gracie," he said, leaning over the counter. "Can you answer a question for me?"

"Sure, what's up?" I asked, anxiously looking at the long line forming behind Patrick.

"So Dr. Hollis is your dad, right? Somebody said he was."

"Yes, he's my dad," I said cautiously, not sure where this was going.

"Why would he be listed on the tournament program as Dr. John Markley?" His face wrinkled up in a look of genuine puzzlement. "It's him. I mean, that name's on the Riverside's website, with his picture. The guy was my professor."

I could not for the life of me come up with a brilliant excuse. Not even a dumb excuse. All that filled my brain was frustration with my dad. There had been many opportunities along the way to stop this situation from happening, and my dad hadn't done anything.

"Well, that's weird." I pointedly looked around him at the long line. "I'm sorry, Patrick, it's getting really busy in here, so I'll need you to move on. Your coffee will be at the pickup window soon. Best of luck today."

Looking annoyed that his question hadn't been answered, Patrick moved over to the pickup window.

As soon as I could take a break, I went to the back room, got my purse and my burner phone, and told Chloe, Rose, and Beck I needed to go get my water bottle, which I'd left in the car this morning.

I slid into my front seat and hit the phone contact for the agents. Jeremy answered after two rings.

"Hey, Gracie. What's up?"

I told him that Patrick had noticed my dad's new name on the program. And I may have vented a bit about my dad, and the agents themselves, not taking the threat seriously.

"I understand your concern," Jeremy said, after letting me rant. "Your father should have said he recognized the name when he saw the list of potential players. Let's not panic. I will talk to Maura and the other marshals. We'll come up with a plan."

I hung up feeling a little relieved that Jeremy was now taking this seriously. My biggest worry was that Patrick was an unpredictable person. I had no idea what he'd say about this—or to whom.

After a busy day, Rose closed and locked the front door at 2:30 p.m. I shut things down in the front area and did a quick wipe down of tables, while Beck carefully loaded her frosted cake into the carrier with the molded chocolate decorations—which she wouldn't let me see yet.

"Do I have to wait till we get to The Riverside to see it?" I said, holding the door open for her.

Beck gave me a mysterious look. "I didn't want to set it up again in the bakery. So yes, you'll have to wait."

When we got to The Riverside, a couple of the players standing outside opened the door for us.

"It's the cake lady!" Aiden McAlister said, as he and

Kenneth Chen bowed low in front of her. "We are not worthy!" Beck laughed and blushed.

I went back to the kitchen, where Martin, one of Chef Jorge's assistants, pulled out the display case, which had been cleaned out from yesterday's cake.

Beck asked if she could have some space to assemble the cake, and Martin brought her to a spot to the side, next to a sink and counter.

"Beck, I'm going to try to find my dad or Reggie. You good?"

She nodded and went to work.

I found my dad sitting on a barstool, sipping an ale and listening intently to one of the older players in the tournament, a man with a drawn face, heavy black glasses, and a salt-and-pepper beard. Derek Bartolo. Reggie had pointed him out to me yesterday.

I went up to the bar to join them.

"Derek, this is my daughter, Gracie. Her bakery, The Laughing Loaf, is catering the tournament lunches."

Derek nodded solemnly. "Good to meet you, Gracie. That naan sandwich was very good. Are you a chess player like your father?"

"I'm a terrible chess player." I groaned ruefully. "My dad tried to teach me growing up, but I never got that whole strategy thing."

"At least you know *how* to play. It's a good game for critical thinking. Unfortunately, the chess world is changing. The credibility of the players nowadays—" He threw up his hand and grimaced. "Players are training on AI and it's taken all the creativity out of the game. You might as well be a software program, not a reasoning human being."

I thought about what Patrick Bowman had said at the bakery this morning. Could Andrew Mehta or other players at this tournament be using technology to do the thinking for them? Was that considered cheating?

With a nod to my dad, Derek Bartolo drained the last of his drink and slid off the barstool. He mumbled a "nice to meet you," and headed out to the dining area.

"That was interesting." I turned toward my dad. "Is he right about chess players using computers to figure out the moves for them?"

"It's a complicated issue, Gracie. Mehta, Younghee, and the rest of the players here have played chess for years. They've played more matches than I can imagine. They could use AI to figure out some strategies. It's often used as a learning tool. And for kids getting into chess, who don't have a lot of financial resources, it's an affordable way to get better at the game."

"But players here at the tournament wouldn't be using it during the games, would they?" I asked.

My dad laughed and shook his head. "You can use software to cheat in online games. At this tournament, we are playing *in real life*, IRL, as the kids say. Two people playing at a table, in person, like we're doing here, is called over-the-board playing—OTB. The only way someone could cheat here would be if they smuggled in a cell phone or electronic device. That has happened at tournaments. But Reggie and I are diligent about checking for these things."

"What would make Derek say that then?"

My dad took another sip of his ale.

"Honestly?" My dad smiled to himself. "Derek thinks if he can't win, it must be because the other players are cheating."

I told him about Patrick Bowman at the bakery, and his claim that he knew how Mehta was able to win. That he'd figured out Mehta's system and was going to beat him at the tournament.

My dad laughed and shook his head. "That is ridiculous. The students I tutor call that 'trash talk.' Patrick Bowman might have beaten Kenneth, but he can't beat Andrew Mehta. He's smart but not in the same league."

"He seemed pretty confident he can win," I said, looking toward the kitchen to see if Beck was coming out with the cake yet. "And he also asked why you had a different name on the tournament program and the Riverside's website." I told him Jeremy was working on a plan to address this.

My dad just nodded, admitted no guilt in the matter, and—big surprise—changed the subject.

"I don't know that you've kept up with the news today, Gracie. We've already had three matches today. Bartolo won his game with Trey Godwin quite easily—I feel a little sorry for the young man. Then Kenneth Chen beat Aiden McAlister. I'm looking forward to a Mehta–Park showdown at the end of today."

I wished I could be there to see it.

Knowing what I did from my chat with Younghee—and Mehta's comment that she was the player he feared most-- this could be a very interesting match indeed.

Chapter Eight

It had been almost forty-five minutes and Beck still hadn't come out of the kitchen with the cake.

I was getting nervous.

I worried that she'd had some kind of *cake-tastrophe*. Maybe her artistic vision for the cake was spoiled by a broken molded decoration or an uneven or collapsed cake layer.

While my dad got up to go in search of Reggie, I stood up and started moving toward the kitchen.

A few seconds later, Beck came out of the kitchen with Reggie, who was pushing the display case.

Reggie was glowing, and Beck's cheeks were pink—maybe from excitement but probably just the result of working in a warm kitchen.

Reggie steered the case into the dining and conversation area and put it into place, setting the brake on the wheels with his foot.

Beck and Reggie both stepped back and stood looking at the cake.

"It's done!" I said excitedly, as I came up to look at the case. Then I saw it.

Just *wow*.

The cake was frosted with dark chocolate frosting, and situated around the circumference of the cake were five molded chocolate redwood trees, with bark in reddish brown grooves that looked remarkably realistic. Beck had nailed the texture.

Sprinkled across the middle of the top of the cake was a carpet of wispy chocolate pine needles, a few tiny pinecones amid them. Two players, a man and a woman, leaned over a black and red chess board laid out on a round, flat redwood stump.

The look on both of their faces was intense: they were fierce competitors, snarling at each other. The chess board was a square of chocolate, painted in white and dark brown chess board squares. Tiny chess pieces sat on the board; the pieces were lined up on both sides of the board as if it were the beginning of a game.

This was a cake, but it was also a sculpture. The forest setting was calm and picturesque, but the chess players leaning over the board brought a tenseness and animosity that was a stark contrast with the peaceful forest setting.

"Beck, this is incredible." I didn't know what else to say. Beck had captured deep emotion in this tableau. It wasn't in any way cute. It was striking and artistic.

And unsettling.

Reggie turned to Beck, looking unable to put his appreciation into words. So, as if he were Paul Hollywood on *The Great British Baking Show*, he reached out and shook her hand.

"Thank you," he said simply. "This is perfection."

Beck turned to me, her eyes bloodshot.

"Gracie, I'd like to get back to the bakery. I have prep to do. If you'll let me, I'd like to go home a little early. I'm so tired."

I hugged her. "Of course. We've got Chloe till closing. She can pitch in with cleanup and prep."

On the drive back to the bakery, Beck told me how hard it had been last night, molding and painting the cake decorations, when she was trying hard not to fall asleep.

"Do you feel Reggie paid you fairly for the hours you put into this?" Beginning bakers often underprice their work, afraid to charge too much. I'd done that.

Beck turned to me, her eyes big. "Yes! I wanted to give some of it back, but he wouldn't let me."

That sounded very much like Beck—and also very much like Reggie. He knew the full worth of what he'd received from her.

Sam picked Beck up at 2:30 p.m., and I helped her carry her boxes and tote the bags of equipment out to the car. I told her I'd call Sam to make sure she actually did go to bed early.

Earlier that day, Reggie and my dad extended an invitation to me and Nate to join the chess players for the dinner banquet. Mary Jo volunteered to come to the house to watch Biga, who was starting to warm up to her.

Since the dinner was semiformal, I wore the black dress with the sash that I'd worn in my Seattle days. At 6:30, not long after he'd returned from his coastal shoot and taken a shower, Nate came by to pick me up, wearing his grey three-piece suit which was his one formal outfit. It looked vintage, out of date in a hip, retro way—like something a posh prep schooler would have worn in the '70s.

"That *dress*." Nate couldn't stop smiling a goofy smile and looking at me as we got ready to go out to his car. "Do you know what you're going to do to those young chess nerds wearing that?"

This was my LBD—a sleeveless little black dress. An LBD was always appropriate for gatherings like this. I didn't have to match anything or put on multiple items or even think about it. I always thought men had it easy: all they needed was a button-down shirt, a tie, and slacks, and they were set. This dress was my easy option, my version of that uniform.

My dad had already gone over to The Riverside, since he and Reggie were planning some kind of pep talk at dinner.

With a few minutes to spare before Mary Jo arrived, Nate and I kissed and cuddled a bit on the sofa, then got into a discussion over whether dogs could feel remorse. I said at some level, yes. Nate disagreed. We ended up laughing over how seriously we were taking the discussion. When Mary Jo came to the door, we turned Biga over to her, and the two had a moment of checking each other out.

Biga sniffed at her, then started nuzzling her arm. I guess she passed the test.

Nate and I took off in his Volvo. Though it had been a long day, I was energized and excited to spend time with the players tonight.

WE ENTERED THE RIVERSIDE, where the lights were dimmed, and a swing dance band played in an area set up in front of the fireplace. It was fun, lively music and it made me want to dance with my boyfriend—who, unlike me, actually knew how to do this kind of dancing.

My dad saw us come in and excitedly headed our way, from where he'd been talking to Reggie near the bar.

"Good to see you, Nate," my dad said, smiling at him. "Gracie, I thought I'd let you know the latest. Mehta and Park's 5:15 p.m. match ended in a draw."

"How does this affect their chances of winning the tournament?" I asked.

"They each earn a half a point for the draw," he said. "Everyone was predicting Mehta would win. Of course, it will depend on their other pairings. We still have two other rounds to play in this tournament."

I'd hoped Younghee would win, though I suppose a draw was better than a loss. And probably showed the two were closely matched.

I looked over at the dining area to see the long dining table now decorated with a black tablecloth and crisp white runner, highlighted with a centerpiece of white roses and black dahlias.

Reggie stood near the table, waving for my dad to join him. My dad excused himself.

"Nate, you have to see Beck's cake." I steered us in the opposite direction, to the display case in the lunch area, where a growing group of players and their wives had gathered. "It's crazy good. She's outdone herself this time."

We waited till some of the onlookers started heading to the dining table. A few of the players had come up to take pictures of each other in front of the cake. Kenneth Chen and Aiden McAlister posed, leaning toward each other, and trying to scowl like the chess players on the cake, while Rich Haskins took their picture with his phone.

Nate walked around the sides of the case to look at the cake, studying it from a few different angles.

"Beck did this?" His eyes softened as he studied it. "I can't believe this is a cake."

I looked in at the two chess players, the man and the woman, leaning over the board, glaring.

"A fierce competition." I leaned into Nate as we studied the cake. "Which seems about right. Most of the players seem focused on beating one person."

"Andrew Mehta?"

I told him in a low voice what both Younghee Park and Patrick Bowman had told me this morning.

"This is going to be interesting," Nate said. "So the winner is whoever gets the most points from all their matches. And we'll know that on Monday morning."

"It sounds like Mehta and Park are pretty far ahead so far."

"I'd like to watch the final matches on Monday morning," Nate said as he leaned in to look at the detail on the cake. "Do you think there's room in the observation area?"

"Apparently, it's called the *skittles* area. Players and observers watch matches, discuss them, and sometimes play each other informally there. You're registered to play in the community tournament that day. I don't see why they wouldn't let you in."

The band stopped playing and Reggie went onto the stage to pick up a microphone. He lifted a champagne glass and took a sip.

"Welcome to the second night of the River Grove Chess Tournament. At this point in the weekend, I've watched you all play. Everyone here is a winner based on the performances I saw. Tonight, we are celebrating our top winners: Andrew Mehta and Younghee Park's match ended in a stalemate, still leaving them at the top. Patrick Bowman and Maya Singh have moved up in the standings. Congratulations to you all."

Reggie took a look at the notes in front of him. "I want

to call special attention to our cake on display, which you'll be enjoying for dessert tonight. The artistic creations you saw yesterday and today in the display case were made by talented River Grove baker, Beck Rodriguez. Let's have a hand for her."

A loud round of applause thundered through The Riverside with a few scattered and enthusiastic *woots*.

"It's time to make your way to our banquet table. Look for your place card. And enjoy Chef Jorge's dinner tonight: osso bucco, roasted root vegetables, and pistachio-panzanella salad. Enjoy."

Nate and I found our place cards near the end of the long table, next to my father and across from Andrew Mehta.

My dad turned to greet Trey Godwin, who was seated next to him, and ask about a particular move he'd made in his match yesterday. Trey explained, as his pale, spindly hands traced movements on the tablecloth as if on a chess board. He had not done well in the tournament so far, and he looked unhappy tonight.

After I sat down, I looked around and spotted Younghee Park, seated on Mehta's side of the table. She shot a nervous, assessing glance over at Mehta, who was staring dully at his plate and didn't notice her. Mehta looked very tired and had brought a half-finished cosmopolitan with him from the bar.

My father introduced me and Nate to the champion.

"Andrew, this is my daughter Gracie, whose bakery catered the lunches here. And this is her boyfriend, Nate Behrens."

I nodded to the young chess champion. "Glad to meet you. Best of luck in the tournament, Andrew."

Nate nodded. "I hope to see you play your big match tomorrow."

Shadows circled Mehta's eyes. He looked like he'd rather be somewhere, anywhere else than at this table.

"Nice to meet you both." He nodded and began eating his dinner.

My father, not one for observing social cues, leaned over the table in Mehta's direction and launched into a play-by-play of Mehta's game with Younghee this afternoon, periodically asking why he'd made certain moves.

Mehta looked blearily at my dad as he talked, his eyes occasionally straying to his plate or down the table at other attendees.

I nudged my dad's side with my elbow, but of course he didn't get the hint.

I leaned over to whisper to him. "Dad, I think Reggie had a question for you."

My father cut short his play by play. "Really?" He looked around to locate Reggie, who was standing near the kitchen. "Then I'll be right back."

Mehta let out a long sigh as he watched my father get up and leave. "Thank you," he breathed in my direction.

I smiled sympathetically. "You look like you've had a hard day."

Nate nodded at Mehta. "Chess is John's passion. Sometimes he gets so excited about it, he doesn't pick up on social cues."

"I'm sorry if I was rude to him," Mehta said wearily, looking years older than a recent college graduate. "Today's been--overwhelming. I need to go upstairs soon to get rest for tomorrow."

Meanwhile, Younghee was now animatedly chatting with the player across the table from her, Aiden McAlister.

"Good luck in your games tomorrow," Nate said to Mehta.

I couldn't say that, because at this point, I was on Team Younghee. Since she and Maya were outnumbered in this tournament, I was rooting for them.

Mehta poked at the osso bucco on his plate with a fork, gave up on it, then went on to finish his salad.

He finally set down his fork and pushed his chair back. He rubbed his forehead and closed his eyes.

"I'm going upstairs," Mehta said to me. "I've enjoyed meeting you. And thanks for the rescue." His mouth turned up in a half smile.

With that, the biggest attraction at the River Grove Chess Tournament left the banquet and headed for the stairs. Not that I was curious—but of course I was—I turned to see Younghee's eyes follow him up the stairs.

A few minutes later, my father came back, looking confused. "Well, it turns out Reggie didn't need to talk to me after all. With everything going on, I think he completely forgot what he needed to ask me."

Nate and I connected with a glance at each other and tried to look normal.

"I'm not surprised," Nate said with a shrug. "You're both so busy with tournament details."

My dad looked at the empty spot across from us. He looked suddenly downcast.

"Where did Andrew go?"

"He said he needed to get sleep for tomorrow's big match," I said. "He said he had a hard day."

My dad sighed. "I was looking forward to asking him a question about a gambit he set up in his game with Park. It was completely out of the blue. I'll try to catch him after his match tomorrow."

We finished our dinner, chatting with the players and their significant others seated around us. Martin from the kitchen staff wheeled the case with Beck's redwood cake over to the table. He opened it and carefully took the decorations off the cake. He began slicing the cake and plating pieces for the staff to hand out.

I found out Derek Bartolo's wife, Kendra, was in the middle of learning how to bake sourdough and was having disappointing results—I texted her my go-to sourdough recipe and starter routine on the spot. Nate talked to Derek about softball, since Kendra brought up that Derek was on his community team. But Derek was in a bad mood after a conversation with Mehta, who he said brushed him off earlier. He didn't want to talk about softball.

After dinner and a slice of Beck's cake, the swing band returned to their setup by the fireplace.

When the jumping music started, Nate slipped his hand into mine. He whispered in my ear, sounding like a teenaged boy at a prom.

"Hey, you wanna dance?"

I followed him to the dance floor, which Reggie's staff had opened up by pushing furniture in the dining area off to the side.

"As usual, I have no idea what I'm doing out here," I said in his ear.

"Follow me," Nate said, pulling my arm toward him and spinning me around so I felt slightly dizzy. The skirt of my black dress flared out as I spun. I felt free and weightless.

"Hold on to my hands," he said, with an encouraging smile. "I'll do the work."

He pulled me toward him, and he put his arm on my shoulder while I held his other hand. When he moved toward me, I moved back, then he pulled me toward him, and I followed. It felt smooth and easy. Then he spun me, and I held onto his hand and flared out away from him, then he pulled me back in again. I felt like I was flying.

At the end of the song, he pulled me toward him and whispered in my ear in a way that made me melt.

"Nicely done."

I wanted to do anything but go back to the table and make conversation.

The Bartolos got up from their seats to look at the cake decorations, lying on a plate in front of Reggie's spot at the head of the table.

I saw Kendra nudge her husband and say in a low voice, "I think the look on their faces is very accurate, don't you? In fact, I've seen that look on *you*."

Derek Bartolo snarled and pulled away from her.

"You don't get it, do you? It's like being in a war. That's what the game was modeled after when it was invented centuries ago. It's still that way."

Kendra rolled her eyes. "Sometimes a game is just a game, Derek. You don't seem to know where to draw the line."

Nate raised his eyebrows in a questioning look. I nodded toward the table. We walked back to our seats. Since we'd finished with dinner, my father had moved down the table to where Younghee had been sitting. He started talking across the table with Aiden McAlister.

I looked around the room. I hadn't seen Younghee for a while. I wondered if, like Mehta, she was tired and wanted to get rest before tomorrow's matches.

While Nate got us drinks at the bar, I started talking to Kendra Bartolo, who'd returned to the table alone.

"How's your time at the tournament going, Kendra?" I

asked with a friendly smile. "Are you two doing anything else while you're in town?"

She looked around the room, as if checking the whereabouts of her husband. She shook her head.

"It's not going great. Derek feels like he has no chance of winning the tournament with Mehta around. I'm hoping we can leave early and drive up to the wine country tomorrow." She had a wistful look on her face. "We always seem happier when we're wine tasting."

"There are wineries right here in the Santa Cruz Mountains," I said. "Reggie's got a map of some good local ones."

She smiled, but behind her smile, I saw worry. Or was it fear? She scanned the room distractedly. "Thanks, Gracie. Maybe I will ask Reggie."

I glanced around the large room, filled with people chatting and drinking, some still dancing to the swing band.

Rich Haskins and his wife laughed together as they headed toward the stairs, both carrying glasses of champagne and looking tipsy. Rich stifled a yawn.

When my dad talked about his experience with tournaments, he said what surprised him most was how exhausting it was to play even three matches in a day. The intense concentration took a physical toll.

As I looked up to the big wooden stairs that led up to The Riverside's guest rooms, I saw Younghee standing at the top of the stairs, a look of worry on her face.

And it wasn't a look like: *Oh, no, I've misplaced my room key.*

Since Nate was still at the bar, I looked up at her, then got up to meet her on the stairs.

"Younghee, are you okay?"

She looked at me, her eyes puffy and lined with red.

"I'm worried about Drew. I went to his room and

knocked. I heard some movement. So he—or somebody—is in there. I texted him but didn't hear anything."

I swallowed, then thought about how to put this to Younghee. "You weren't on great terms, from what you told me before. Could he be avoiding you?" The possibility I couldn't mention: *Maybe he has someone in his room and you're the last person he'd want to open the door to.*

She looked down the hall toward his room. "Maybe. But he did not look good tonight. I guess—when he didn't answer, it made me worry."

But I'd thought the same thing as I'd sat across from Mehta. He wasn't doing well.

I looked around for Reggie. He was talking to Patrick Bowman near the kitchen. Patrick seemed very happy, which made sense. He'd been doing well so far in the tournament. Maybe I'd judged him too harshly. He was a higher caliber player than I thought.

I could be wrong, but my gut told me Reggie would excuse himself from talking to Patrick, looking for a way out of his conversation with the intense young player.

I got up and made my way to Reggie. When he saw me coming, Reggie put his hand on Patrick's shoulder.

"I've got to speak to Gracie here. Congratulations on your victories, and best of luck tomorrow," he said with a brief smile, dismissing the young man.

As Patrick walked away, I leaned in toward Reggie.

"This may be out of an abundance of caution, but Younghee Park is worried about Andrew Mehta. We both noticed he wasn't looking well tonight. She knocked on his door and got no answer. And he didn't respond when she texted him. Can you check on him?"

"He looked ill earlier—or just tired. With the matches he has tomorrow, he might have taken a sleeping pill to get some rest." He paused for a moment. "It couldn't hurt to check in on him."

I nodded to Younghee, who had returned to her seat. She'd been watching us.

Reggie and I walked up the stairs to the second-floor guest rooms. He tapped on the door, first quietly. After a minute or two wait, he knocked more urgently.

"Andrew, this is Reggie. Checking to see you're okay. I heard you weren't feeling well."

We waited. I leaned in toward the door to see if I could hear any movement.

Silence.

Reggie pulled his keychain out of his pocket, a big old-fashioned iron ring with multiple keys on it.

He knocked and we both stood still, our ears straining to hear any sound in the room.

Distantly, the band had started up again after a break. We were right above them. The beat of the drums vibrated the floor under my feet.

He knocked again. "Andrew, are you there? Just doing a check, since a few people mentioned you were not feeling well."

Reggie put his ear up to the door. He found a key on his chain and slid it into the lock. He turned the doorknob and pushed in, but it stopped at about three inches open. The chain of a sliding lock rattled.

"Did you hear a rasping sound?" Reggie asked, tension in his voice. "Someone trying to breathe."

I heard the sound, very faintly. Then it stopped.

Incredibly quickly, Reggie took a rubber band out of his pocket and slid his hand through the narrow opening of the door. He felt around, closing his eyes as he felt for the round nob on the chain, slipping the rubber band end around it.

Finally, he pulled his hand back. He shut the door, then when he opened it, the rubber band slid the round knob back.

The chain dropped open and hit the back of the door with a *thwack* and a rattle.

Reggie quickly pushed open the door and we hurried in.

The covers crumpled around him, Andrew Mehta lay sprawled on the bed, a knife in his chest.

Chapter Nine

"Riverside Saloon. Second floor—room 8," I croaked into my phone as I talked to the 911 operator. "No pulse. He's not breathing."

Reggie stood pale and slightly slumped over as he looked down at Mehta's body. He took off his sunglasses, and I saw a rare glimpse of the saloon owner's brown eyes, small and squinting. He stood blinking, as if unsure of what he was seeing on the bed.

I looked around the room, my heart pounding. For a few seconds, time seemed to have stopped, and my eyes captured quick snapshots of scenes around the room. A cell phone and champagne glass sat on the antique nightstand next to the bed, along with a watch, cufflinks, and a wallet. A narrow door, which I assumed was the room's closet, wasn't completely closed. The curtains were open, over windows that I was pretty sure were sealed shut.

A suitcase was open on a stand near the bathroom door, revealing neatly folded shirts and slacks.

Five minutes later, boots pounded up the stairs.

The EMTs quickly surrounded Mehta and went to

work, as Reggie and I stepped out of the room and watched from the hallway. I turned around to see Nate standing behind me, a warm, solid presence.

It didn't take long for them to assess the situation. They backed off, and one of the EMTs talked into his radio.

"Adult male, deceased. Knife wound to the chest." I couldn't decipher the response coming back at him on the radio, but after conferring with each other, two of them pulled out a stretcher and prepared to take Mehta away.

I turned away from the doorway. I didn't need to see another one of these. The slowness of the EMTs' movements said it all. There was no urgency.

No hope.

Reggie stepped back from the doorway and tapped my shoulder.

"I want to stay here with the EMTs. Please tell everyone I'll make an announcement when I come downstairs."

I turned around to face Nate. "I'm going back to the table. I want to be with my dad when he hears this."

"Let's go." He reached down and held my hand.

There was a low, dull roar as banquet guests leaned over the tables talking. They'd all seen the EMTs rush up the stairs. All eyes were fastened on Nate and me as we came down the stairs.

We took our seats at the table.

"So what happened up there?" Kendra Bartolo, still sitting by herself, asked me sharply.

"What's going on?" Kenneth Chen said, sitting next to his wife, Carrie, whom I'd met earlier.

I stood up at the end of the table. As people figured out I was going to speak, they hushed.

"Reggie will come down soon and fill everyone in," I

said firmly, as calmly as I could, even though my legs felt wobbly and my knees felt like they would give out. "He knows more than I do."

My father was studying my face, trying to deduce what happened. I couldn't tell him Andrew Mehta was dead. The young champion had been the highlight of the tournament for him. I looked around for Younghee. She was sitting by herself on a barstool, sipping a drink.

I thought about the possibilities. I couldn't imagine Mehta doing this to himself; it must be murder. The question was who? Derek Bartolo, who'd been complaining about Mehta during the tournament, was missing. Younghee Park, spurned girlfriend and Mehta's biggest competition in the tournament, was avoiding everyone at the table and drinking alone.

Patrick, strangely, was dancing by himself, jerking his body around in the dance area maybe in a kind of victory dance, as the swing band played on by the fireplace.

How did someone get into Mehta's locked, chained room to kill him?

Since my father was looking nervous and scared, I squeezed Nate's hand, let it go, then went to sit by him.

As I pulled out the chair next to him, Chief Westerman and Deputy Brad Castro came through The Riverside's front door. My father saw them, too.

"Now I know something's wrong." My dad swallowed and looked me in the eye, maybe thinking he could figure out by my reaction what happened.

I gave a quick nod and pressed my lips together. "You're right."

He glanced around the room and frowned. "Bartolo is gone. Mehta is gone. Something has happened to one of them. I see all the other players."

I nodded. "This will not be good news. Reggie will be down soon to tell us more details."

As we waited, the roar of the crowd at the table grew louder. Guests wanted to know what was going on, and since they didn't know, they speculated. I heard snippets of their conversations.

"Bartolo was jealous of Mehta. Who knows what he did."

"Some intruder shot Mehta. This town is small, but I heard there's a very high crime rate."

"Mehta looked sick. I'm sure it was a medical emergency. He looked awful in his matches today."

Within five minutes, Reggie came down, his footsteps heavy on the steps. I think his timing had something to do with the fact that the EMTs were just about to bring Mehta down on a stretcher.

Reggie walked to the head of the table and directed our attention away from the stairs and toward Beck's cake.

The band had stopped playing and members were now putting away their equipment.

"I'd like to have everyone's attention. We've had an unfortunate incident this evening," Reggie said, pausing. He spoke loudly but calmly. As he started, I snuck a sideways glance at the stairs, where EMTs were now descending with the stretcher.

Reggie stood in front of us, his face more ghostly white than usual. "I'm sorry to tell you, our friend Andrew Mehta is dead."

Gasps and chatter broke out at the table. My father's face crumpled. His lips trembled as he looked down at the table.

"Quiet, please," Reggie said firmly. "I need to tell you

that the police have just arrived. They'll need to talk to each of you tonight before you go to your rooms."

This caused a new round of gasps and conversations around the table.

"Please stay in the downstairs area until you have your chance to talk to Chief Westerman and Deputy Castro. When you're asked, come up the back stairs, right past the kitchen, to the conference room, where they'll be conducting interviews. Drake, from the bar, will show you the way up."

I watched Reggie walk past the bar. The chief and Brad escorted him up the stairs to be interviewed.

At this point, Patrick Bowman had wandered back from the dance area, sweat covering his face. He slunk down into a chair at the end of the table and put his head in his hands.

My father did not look good. As he usually did when he was flustered, he coughed and wiped his lips fastidiously with his napkin.

"I'm so sorry, dad." He was not a touchy-feely person, but he didn't pull away when I put my arm around his shoulder.

"He didn't look well. I assumed he was ill. But this—" He looked at me, his eyes watery behind his glasses. "This sounds like murder, Gracie. We've been through this before. This feels familiar."

I reached for his hand and held it. "I don't see any other possibility. There are a few people who were not happy with Mehta. But there's also a lot I don't know about him."

My dad shook his head. "I wanted this weekend to be a celebration. All of us playing a game we love."

My dad and Reggie had been excitedly planning this tournament for months. They knew and had connected with every player here. The scary thing was that any one of them could have stabbed Andrew Mehta. No one but the players and their families or Beck, my dad, Nate and me had been allowed in The Riverside for this event.

On the other side of me, Nate was talking to Kendra Bartolo, who was dabbing her eyes with a napkin.

"I'm scared. I don't know where Derek is," she said between sobs. "He took off right after dinner. I know he was still upset about losing." I watched as she stopped, frowned, and looked down at the table, glassy-eyed. Was she wondering if her husband was responsible for Mehta's death?

Within fifteen minutes, Reggie returned to the table. The chief and Brad stood by the bar, looking over at our table as they conferred.

Brad came up to our end of the table first.

"Gracie, come on upstairs, please." He gestured, holding his tablet.

The chief waved my father aside, to follow him. "John, come with me. We'll talk in Reggie's office."

The two of us followed the law enforcement team up the back stairs.

The chief took my dad into Reggie's office and shut the door.

"Sit down, Gracie," Brad told me unceremoniously when we reached the conference room outside of Reggie's office. Brad plopped down on a purple papasan chair opposite my seat on the couch.

I let out a sigh and closed my eyes. After everything that had happened, it was a relief to leave the noise and speculative chatter downstairs.

"Gracie. I want you to tell me everything that happened

tonight, from when you came into The Riverside to when you went upstairs with Reggie to Mehta's room." He sat up in the papasan chair and pushed the button on his micro recorder.

I told him about Younghee's concern for Mehta. And how she said she'd heard movement in his room when she'd gone up to knock. And that my dad and I noticed that the chess champion didn't look well at dinner. I'd alerted Reggie after talking to Younghee and he and I had gone up together.

"Did you hear anything upstairs? Any noise when you were in the hall outside his door?"

I had, I suddenly remembered. "Before we entered the room, I heard sort of a gasp coming from inside. It was very quiet."

"That's it?" He sounded disappointed. "You didn't hear anything in the hallway upstairs?"

"Reggie might have noticed more," I tried to remember what else I noticed, but I couldn't think of anything.

"How did you and Reggie get into the room?" Brad asked.

I told him about Reggie unlocking the door with the room key from his key ring. I remembered Reggie's clever rubber band trick when he'd seen the chain lock was on.

"Reggie reached in and slid a rubber band around part of the lock. So when he closed the door again, the rubber band snapped back, and the lock dropped out of the slide."

Brad's eyes widened with excitement. "No way. I saw that trick on TikTok. It's amazing." Then he put on his stern detective face again. "Then he opened the door?"

I nodded. "We saw Mehta right away, in the bed. With the knife in him. Reggie felt for his pulse and his breathing. That's when I called 911."

"Anything else you noticed in the room?" Brad looked at me expectantly. I remembered my first glances around the room. I was so shocked by what I saw—and admittedly because I knew how much Mehta's death would upset my dad. I'd looked around the room randomly, at anything but Mehta.

I pictured the room in my mind. "I guess I saw a few things. On the nightstand there was a phone, a watch and wallet, and a wine glass—no, maybe it was a champagne glass. There was a narrow little closet catty-corner to the main door and there was a shirt on a hanger on the door-knob. His suitcase was open on a stand near the bathroom."

"That's a lot of detail," Brad nodded admiringly. "Any-thing else you noticed about Andrew Mehta that day—or when you met him? When was it, yesterday?"

"He was sitting in the dining area talking to my dad and my dad introduced us. My dad was in awe of Andrew, and he was always trying to get time with him, to ask him about his strategies. Andrew didn't look well yesterday—his phone buzzed. He picked it up and read a text. He looked upset, and then he told my dad he had to go. He had something he had to do for somebody."

Brad typed this into his tablet. "Any idea who texted him?"

"You or the chief should ask my dad. I didn't see, but my dad was right next to Andrew. He might have seen some-thing on his phone."

Brad typed this into his tablet.

"Anything else?"

"Do you want to know anything I noticed about other players at the tournament and what they said about Mehta?"

Brad visibly mulled this over. "Sure, I guess. Even if it might not seem related to his death."

First, I told him that Derek Bartolo's wife said he was missing and had disappeared during dinner. I told him about Bartolo's rant about Mehta in his conversation with me and my dad.

I told him about Patrick Bowman, and how he said he'd figured out Mehta's game. And how he was going to, "beat him to a pulp."

At that, Brad let out a swear word. He began typing on his tablet.

I continued.

"He said Mehta was going to 'learn what it feels like to lose.'"

And, reluctantly, I told him that Mehta and Younghee used to be a couple and that it had not ended well.

Brad grunted and shook his head. "Guess I asked the right question, huh?"

"I listen in when I shouldn't. People tend to unload on me. That must be what it is," I said, shrugging my shoulders.

With that, Brad said I was free to go back downstairs. My dad was still in with the chief. I got up from the couch and headed downstairs, suddenly exhausted. What I'd seen tonight had sucked the remaining energy out of me.

I joined Nate at the table.

"That didn't take long," Nate said, reaching for my hand under the table.

"Brad and the chief are splitting up the interviews," I said. "I told Brad everything I'd seen, and even what I'd heard from a few people who had possible motives for wanting to get rid of Mehta."

He looked at the empty seat next to him. "Kendra Bartolo went looking for her husband. She seemed worried

—maybe afraid he took his anger out on Mehta. From what he's been saying, she's right to worry."

"I hope she's a calming influence on him," I said, scanning The Riverside's cavernous downstairs. "I hope he's only been out for a walk in the woods to blow off steam."

"Yeah," he said with a grim look. "Me, too."

Reggie's staff had cleared off the table and were putting out plates stacked with my red-and-black chess board cookies.

In a few minutes, Drake came up to the table and asked for Nate and Trey Godwin to go upstairs to be interviewed. Trey stood up, pushed his chair in, and followed the bartender.

"I'll see you soon." Nate put a hand on my shoulder and then headed up the back stairs, just as my father came down. He looked drained and suddenly very old.

I looked over to see Younghee still at the bar, slunk down in her seat. I had no idea what she was feeling right now, but it couldn't be good.

I went over to take a seat next to her.

When she turned to me, her eyes were puffy, and her mascara had smeared under her eyes.

"He's dead." She said in a hoarse voice. "I should have known it was coming."

I didn't ask her what she meant. But, because she genuinely seemed heartbroken, I did say: "I'm sorry, Younghee."

She continued crying, and Drake, the bartender always prepared for a sob story, handed her a box of tissues. Younghee blotted her face and took a deep breath.

"We played tournaments together as teenagers. At first, we took turns winning. I was the child prodigy. My dad taught me how to play when I was three. Drew was the up-

and-coming champion. He only learned to play when he was fifteen, and he just got better and better with time. When he was just starting out, everyone already knew me. But eventually I couldn't keep up, and he started surpassing me. We were both very competitive. Sometimes it felt like we were enemies. Well, enemies that respected each other."

"You said you knew it was coming—his death," I said gently. "What did you mean by that?"

She sniffed and blotted her face.

"There's a long line of chess champions who ended up so obsessed with chess, it made them lose their minds. There's a famous quote: 'Poets do not go mad, but chess players do.' It can do that to you. Take over your life.

"When Drew and I were still together, I started to see it. He was always thinking about his next game, what advantage he could get over his competitor. He studied the great players. He used AI simulations and ran through his options constantly—what if I made this move? What about that one? It was like he was on an adrenaline rush with every game he played. He ate ultra healthy foods and took supplements he read about that were supposed to make him think sharper. But they just made him look sick, not well. I think all of that. . . well, it killed him."

I wanted to tell her that no, it was actually a knife that had killed him tonight. But maybe that was what finished him off.

"I wasn't one of the things helping him win." She said, her eyes glazing over. Her face had turned red, probably from the alcohol. "So he let go of me. Didn't return my calls. He avoided me."

"That must have hurt."

Younghee ran her finger around the top of her glass.

"It made me try harder. *Fine,* if he's going to do these

things to get better, I'll work harder at it. It was my form of revenge. I studied up on his games, but it didn't really help much, with that draw today."

"Are you going to tell the police all of this?"

She shrugged then let out an odd little laugh. "What do they know about chess?"

"Probably not much."

I watched Younghee finish the last of her drink. I sensed this was not about chess as much as hurt and betrayal. A universal feeling, whether you've been ditched for another lover, or the love of money as in the case of my ex.

I went back to the table to see how my father was doing. He and Nate were sitting next to each other talking.

"You and Nate don't have to stay." My father looked up at me tiredly, his eyes bleary. "You're done with your interviews. Reggie and I have a lot to discuss tonight. We have to decide whether we want to continue with the tournament. I'll be back late."

I had to get up early tomorrow morning. But I didn't feel comfortable ditching my dad. Then Nate stepped in.

"John, give me a call when you're done," Nate said firmly. "I'll come back and pick you up."

I let out a sigh of relief. I didn't want my dad to try to drive home by himself, especially after the shock he'd had tonight. His vision wasn't as good at night.

"Dad, call Nate." I could see my dad mulling through rebuttals to this plan. "Do it. Or I won't sleep—and I really need to."

He pursed his lips and nodded. "Very well. I'll call him."

. . .

Nate pulled up to our house and walked me up to the door. Mary Jo and my little dog peeked out the curtain at us.

He held me for a while, then gave me a kiss on the cheek.

"Why does it feel weird to kiss after a murder?" he asked with such solemnity, I let out a nervous laugh.

"Thank you for giving my dad a ride. He's having a hard time."

"That's why I offered. I kind of care about the guy."

"Another thing I love about you." I reached up to give him a kiss on the cheek. Since he was a foot taller than me, it was quite a reach. "Be careful out there."

"I will." He planted a kiss on my forehead. "You don't need to worry about me."

As soon as I unlocked and opened the door, Biga ran to me, acting like Mary Jo had tortured him in my absence. The opposite was probably true: she spoiled him.

I picked him up and cuddled him, while my dad's girlfriend stood up from the couch, rubbed her eyes, and yawned.

"Thank you, Mary Jo. How was the boy?"

"He was so sweet. Just sat curled up next to me on the couch while I read. He gave me those puppy dog eyes, trying to get food out of me, and it worked. I gave him some of the treats you left out."

"What a con job, you little muffin boy." I scolded him and he proceeded to lick my face. "He turns on the cuteness in exchange for food."

"Your father called me and told me what happened— and that he'll be talking with Reggie for a while," Mary Jo said sadly. "He told me he's gutted."

"Nate's driving him back. He shouldn't drive tonight."

"That's smart."

I realized I should invite Mary Jo to stay if she didn't want to go out this late.

"You're welcome to stay here tonight," I told her. "Either in my dad's room or out here on the couch, whatever—uh, works for you." I had no idea what their status was as far as that went, but I wanted to give her options.

"Gracie, that's sweet of you. I'd like to stay to see your father, but I do need to get back to the house. I've got somebody coming by the nursery early."

I thanked her for dog-sitting my pup and carried Biga out to escort Mary Jo to her car.

"Tell your father to call tonight if he's not too tired," she said as she opened her car door. "I want to hear how he's doing."

"We should do lunch sometime soon. I can come over to the theatre in Boulder Creek for a quick lunch." Mary Jo had just gotten a part-time job as an office assistant for a local theatre company—a way to get back to the theatre life she'd left years ago. Which she did in addition to running River Grove's plant nursery, Growing Affection.

I hugged her. We'd come a long way in our relationship in the past year. I used to resent her and compare her to my mother, who'd passed away when I was fifteen. Now I was able to enjoy her for who she was.

"I'd love that, Gracie. Now stay safe."

NATE DIDN'T BRING my dad home till eleven thirty—a little late for me. I lay out on the couch, meaning to wait up for them. Thoughts of the lock and chain on Mehta's door— and who could have possibly gotten into his room—cycled through my head.

How could someone have gotten into Mehta's room if

Reggie had the only key? The windows were sealed shut. The door was locked and chained.

My obsessive thoughts continued for a while, but sleep won out.

Somewhere in there, I remember Nate kissing me, the brush of his whiskers on my face, his woodsy smell, and the rumble of his low, throaty voice.

Chapter Ten

DAY 3
River Grove Chess Tournament
Sunday, August 31

Pairings
****REVISED****

Younghee Park - Trey Godwin
Kenneth Chen - Maya Singh
Rich Haskins - Patrick Bowman
Derek Bartolo - AIden McAlister
(on bye due to loss of player: Gunnar Larsen)

I got up by 5:00 a.m., groggy and with a headache.

I poked my head into my dad's room to see him asleep. I hoped he had gotten rest and some distance from last night's events. I'd check in on him at The Riverside later.

After downing some weak pre-coffee, I lured Biga into his crate and we took off for Sunday morning at the bakery.

The sky was growing lighter. A pink glow silhouetted the trees as I parked the car in the alley and took Biga's crate out of the back hatch of the Subaru.

I wondered what news I'd hear today. I'm sure the chief and Brad had stayed at The Riverside till late last night, searching the room and conducting interviews.

I cuddled with Biga in his pen for a few minutes, getting him to play with his toy, then making him get up on two legs to grab his treat from me. He was his usual perky self, oblivious to what happened last night.

I washed my hands and got to work in the back room, rolling out dough for cinnamon rolls.

I could tell by the look on Beck's face when she came in the back door—lips in a firm line, her eyes red rimmed—she knew what had happened last night, which saved me the trouble of having to break the bad news to her.

Sam was good friends with Nate and with Deputy Brad. I'm sure he'd heard about Mehta's murder from one or the other of them.

She was carrying a wrapped box.

"Good morning, Gracie." She looked just as tired as she had yesterday after her marathon cake-making session the night before. "I had trouble sleeping last night after I heard the news, so I got up and made a cake. Reggie left me a message to make a simple one for today, since they've decided to continue the tournament. Since everyone's still in town, they want to make the best of it."

"Does it help to have something to work on?" I asked as I brought the melted brown sugar, butter, and caramel mixture back to the table to slather on the cinnamon rolls.

She took the three cake layers, frosted with a crumb-coat, out of the box, then yawned and widened her eyes. "It helps a lot. I'm going create something beautiful and—peaceful. Not like yesterday's cake."

In light of the murder, yesterday's cake with its scowling competitors did seem eerily prescient.

Rose came in at 6:30 p.m., donning an apron over what looked like a square dance skirt and ruffly top, in bright red paisley. She pulled the beignet dough out of the fridge and set it on a table, ready to roll it out and slice it into squares.

When she went over to the stove to set up the pot for frying, I took her aside and told her what had happened at The Riverside last night.

"Seriously?" She took in a deep breath and paused. "And there's no chance he could have done it himself?"

"That would have been impossible from what I saw. The police have started a murder investigation." I pulled the phone out of my apron pocket to check if I'd received any other messages—just one I'd received from Reggie a few minutes ago.

> Good morning, my friend. Tournament still on. Lunch service as usual.

"We'll need to have lunch items ready." I thought through what we'd need to get done in order to serve lunch here and at The Riverside. "Can you help get the bread ready? I have sourdough to bake. We'll need to slice and pack. I texted Chloe. She'll come in at seven thirty. She can bake the flatbread for wraps."

"No problem," Rose nodded slowly, looking like she was still absorbing the news. "Let me know. I'll do whatever's needed."

The three of us worked together, focused on our tasks. No music playing since none of us was in the mood to sing.

Each of us worked, head down, wrapped tightly in the comfort of our morning routine.

After Chloe came through the back door, she put on her apron and washed her hands. She pulled the tub of flatbread dough out of the fridge and began rolling it into balls on the floured metal table.

"Good morning, Chloe." I flashed a smile as I passed her on my way to the oven. "I'm sure your grandfather was out late."

She rolled her eyes. She looked tired. "He came back at about 3:00 a.m. and woke up my mom's dog. Then he started yelling at Biff, and the dog wouldn't stop barking. I couldn't get to sleep for a while."

"He didn't make an arrest last night, did he?"

"He seemed really grouchy this morning. That means he didn't."

I'd try to catch up with the chief later today.

"Thanks for coming in today, Chloe. We needed the help this weekend."

"No problem." She let out a tired sigh. "Jeb's been playing online chess this week, so I haven't seen much of him. He's in the community tournament tomorrow and he wants to win bad." She stifled a yawn. "Can I make myself a latte, Gracie?"

With all the times she'd pitched in to work the espresso machine, Chloe was a pro.

"Sure, go ahead. Can you make me one, too?"

She gave me a thumbs up.

I shouldn't be surprised that Jeb was in the community tournament. It would be nice if he ended up playing my dad, who'd tutored him and had become his role model as he prepared to head off to college to study physics.

In case any players came in this morning, I chose a chess joke and set it on its stand. As if anyone could laugh today.

Laughing Loaf Joke of the Day
"My dog plays chess with me."
"Wow, you must have a smart dog."
"Hey, he's not *that* smart. I've won three out of five games."

The crowd was bigger than usual, once we opened the doors. I did see a few familiar faces from the chess tournament—Rich Haskins and his wife, Emma, then Maya Singh and her mother, who came in to try our new chai lattes. The dining area rumbled with conversation. From the snippets I heard, there was a lot of speculation about last night's murder—as people settled in with their pastries and tea and espresso drinks.

Any event that happened—whether it was murder or gossip about a new romance—spread like wildfire in River Grove. The town was like a big family; when you knew everyone, anything that happened to *anyone* was a big deal and you had to hear all the details.

Griff, son of revered 1986 River Grove Chili Cookoff champion Scotty Baxter, came up to the front of the line that morning with a big smile. He was tall and lanky and had the tanned, leathery skin of a man who worked in construction.

"G'morning, Gracie. I heard about what happened at The Riverside last night. One of those chess players from out of town was killed?"

I nodded. "Andrew Mehta was found dead in his room after dinner."

"He just, like, died?" Griff was trying to look casual,

while leaning over to scan the display case. "Do you think he was murdered?"

"I don't know all the details of the case, Griff. The chief and Brad would be the people to ask." I changed the subject. "How's your dad? How's the family?"

Griff's face grew somber. "We're having some trouble with dad. He forgot to turn the water off upstairs, and it flooded. Lots of damage to the floor and ceiling. We don't feel good about leaving him by himself no more. We're looking for someone who can stay with him during the day."

"Really? I'll keep my ears open for someone who might be interested." Scotty was a sweetheart, with a sense of humor and a mischievous bent. Staying with him wouldn't be the worst job someone could take on. There were quite a few River Grovians looking for work right now.

"Thanks, Gracie." He smiled gratefully as I packed a box with beignets for him. "That would be great. You take care now and stay safe."

I handed him the pink box and turned to the next customer.

In half an hour, I went back to work on bread with Rose, who'd decided we needed to hear a playlist of early Johnny Cash hits this morning. She was right. The man's earthy, mournful voice worked out better for our moods this morning than glossy pop songs.

Chloe left to work the front counter. The coffee had perked her up and she was her friendly self.

I heard her chattering with a morose Mayor C. I'm sure she'd been briefed by the chief last night, if not early this morning.

Beck had set her chess cake aside in her work area, frosted with dark chocolate and ready to be topped by decorations, so she could prep the naanini for Chloe to fry up for the tournament lunch.

"How's the cake doing?" I asked as I passed her at the stove.

"It's fine. It's a simple three-layer yellow cake, frosted. That's what Reggie wanted." She glanced back at the cake on its pedestal. "It takes the pressure off, that's for sure. Reggie asked for a specific decoration and it's super easy."

I'd wait and see what this decoration was. I was curious.

"I'd like to head over to The Riverside at ten," I told her. "Will the cake be ready then? I can take it. No rush."

She looked over at the cake, thinking this through. "It should be ready. If it's not too crazy here, we can go together."

"Chloe and Rose should be able to handle things here." I smiled at my assistant manager.

At 9:00 a.m., Chloe poked her head into the back room. I was laying Rose's finished flatbreads into a lined basket. We'd mixed up a double batch, so we'd be covered for lunch here and at the tournament.

"Gracie, the chief wants to talk to you."

"If it's just him, tell him to come back here. I can't take a break right now."

Chloe let out a whoop. "Oh, my God, *yes*. The man needs to hear that more often. Good for you, Gracie."

I hadn't even thought it through. All I knew was that we were busy today. Regardless of what the chief had to say to me, we had a lot to get done, both for lunch at the bakery and at The Riverside.

The chief came in, looked uneasily at my staff, and sat down on a stool next to me. He took in a deep breath.

"Gracie, can you tell your employees to give us a few minutes?"

I nodded at Beck, Chloe, and Rose. They looked at each other, then filed out the door to the front of the bakery.

The chief lowered his voice.

"Gracie, we've got a problem."

Besides a murder? What else could there be?

He swallowed and looked down at his knotted fingers.

"Andrew Mehta's murder." He tightened his lips and looked over at the floury table I continued to work on. "We've gone through everything. Mehta's door was locked from the inside. So were the windows. Reggie had the only other key on his chain, and he swore he had it in his pocket all night."

"What are you saying?" I looked up from the balls of dough I was flattening.

"Nobody could have gotten into that room, aside from Reggie."

The chief lifted his shoulders in an "I give up" gesture.

"Gracie, at this point, I am not sure where to look. As far as I can see, there's no way this murder could have happened."

Chapter Eleven

I could have figured that out.

Only Reggie could have gotten into Mehta's room.

He carried the ring of keys for all the guest rooms at The Riverside.

"Reggie was downstairs the entire time—from when Mehta was eating dinner across from my dad and I, to when I went up to talk to him. After Younghee Park said she was worried about Mehta."

"Yes." The chief said slowly, frowning. "A couple of other guests verified that."

Was the chief thinking that somehow Reggie had done this? How could he even think of him as a possibility? I remembered the look on Reggie's face last night when we got into Mehta's room—a look of utter shock. He'd been devastated.

Yet in a murder case, no one was exempt from consideration. I glanced up at the clock, as I continued to form and flatten balls of flatbread dough. Considering what the chief was saying, it calmed me to keep doing it.

"There's no way the windows could have been opened from the outside?" I pictured the old-fashioned latches on those windows that turned to lock. From what I'd seen of the other rooms at The Riverside, most of these had been painted over and tended to stick—or not open at all.

The chief shook his head slowly. "Even if the windows could be opened from the outside, that side of the building is a straight drop down to the pavement. No drainpipes, no hillside, no places to hang onto. It's too high for any ladder I know of. Brad and I checked it out early this morning."

"There's no way Mehta could have stabbed himself?" I offered up the possibility. "He seemed pretty depressed yesterday." I'd been trying to erase from my mind the sight of Mehta in his bed last night.

The chief shook his head. "I asked the coroner. He said with the angle of the knife, there's no way he could have done it."

"What do you do next, then?" I asked the chief as I laid the flattened pieces of dough onto a baking sheet.

He looked at me, his tired eyes drooping.

"A crime scene team from San Jose will go through the room section by section this afternoon, trying to find any traces someone left behind." The chief rubbed his eyes. "We'll work backwards from there, trying to figure out possible motives. Whoever did this was smart. Too smart."

"And The Riverside is hosting a tournament for very smart people."

"That's what worries me," the chief said, glancing down at his buzzing cell phone. "I'm not sure we have the resources or the manpower to catch someone like that."

The chief should know by now. Saying a case was unsolvable didn't discourage me. It pulled me in.

I started turning the facts of the case over in my brain, playing with the puzzle.

By 9:45 A.M., Beck was boxing up her cake and decorations. She slipped her tools and a tub of buttercream frosting into her tote bag.

Rose had lunch fixings packed up for us to take over.

Then Elise and Daisy would pick up the insulated container with the warm naanini to take over to the Riverside at 11:15.

After loading up my car, Beck and I drove over to The Riverside.

While Beck took her cake and decorating materials into the Riverside's kitchen to finish off the cake, I took a seat at the empty bar.

The saloon's cavernous main room was quiet this morning, except for the background music of light acoustic jazz. A few players from the tournament, some with their significant others, sat at tables in the dining area, looking bleary. They drank coffee and picked at the pastries on their plates. No one talked. I looked around the room for the Bartolos, wondering if Derek had reappeared last night—and if the chief had interviewed him.

I stayed to watch the first match of today's tournament. I'd finally get my chance to see Younghee play. She was paired with Trey Godwin.

I sat in the skittles area, drinking coffee, surrounded by a few of the players. Aiden McAlister and Kenneth Chen also guzzled coffee, looking very tired. Maya Singh's mother sat watching, while Maya diligently took notes.

It was a very short game.

Younghee, playing the white pieces, started by moving

her pawn to the middle of the board, so she was able to free up her bishop and queen. Then she was able to move her queen to within range of the black king. She had a bishop ready to threaten Trey's king, too.

Trey looked flustered. His cheeks burned pink in his pale face. I thought I heard him repeat to himself, "*Damn. I should know this.*"

He looked around the board, then finally moved a pawn, which even *I* knew wasn't going to help him.

Younghee moved her queen, and Trey couldn't defend against it.

Suddenly he stood up stiffly, turned, and walked away, heading for the stairs. He had a blank look on his face.

The spectators in the skittles area applauded Younghee, who looked startled.

"The Scholar's Mate," Aiden McAlister said, watching Younghee with admiration. "Checkmate in four moves. A classic play."

I wanted to go congratulate Younghee, but she quickly grabbed her book and pencil. She walked over to the lunch area and sat down by Gunnar Larsen and his wife.

I walked over to the bar, sat on a stool, and asked Drake for a glass of sparkling water.

Reggie and my dad came down the stairs, both of them looking as if they'd had a late night. Reggie nodded to acknowledge me, then continued on his way to the kitchen.

My dad took a seat next to me at the bar.

"How are things going with the tournament after last night?" I asked.

My dad shrugged. "Reggie and I are trying to plan out the rest of the weekend. We're focusing on just what we need to do. Play out the last two rounds today and tomorrow morning, then set up for the community tournament. We've got twenty players signed up."

"I know that's what you're *doing* today," I said gently. "But how are you feeling? I know how hard last night was for you."

My dad looked down at his hands. The bones on his hands stood out in sharp relief, and the age spots on his skin seemed more pronounced. When you see someone every day, you don't always see the progression of age, its effects. He looked older today.

"Such a loss. Andrew was quite young. I am—well, beside myself. I can't imagine who would do this."

"I'm sorry, dad. Andrew was a brilliant player. He was on his way to greater things." My conversation with Younghee came back to me: Mehta's obsession with chess, how he'd pared his life down to whatever would help him win. At the least, the man hadn't been living a balanced life and had probably veered into self-destructive territory. But now wasn't the time to discuss these things with my dad.

My dad pressed his lips together, a sharp look in his eyes. "What are you going to do about it, Gracie?"

He sat back on the high bar chair, his hands folded on his lap, looking expectant.

If there was one thing my father *wasn't*, it was direct.

"What do you mean?" I asked, knowing exactly what he meant, but I wasn't sure I wanted to hear it. "The chief and Brad are working on it. The chief came over and gave me an update."

"Reggie told me there are some odd circumstances to this murder," he said, his voice lowered.

"The chief told me all about it. The door and windows were locked from the inside. It would have been impossible for anyone to get into the room."

"In the past, you've been able to figure out difficult cases, Gracie." There was a pleading look in his eyes. "You rather liked doing it."

I shrugged. For the past month and a half, I'd enjoyed running my beautifully remodeled bakery without having to snoop around to solve a murder or flee from foreign spies or dissidents.

Last month, I'd been pursued by yet another former client of my ex-husband's secret-selling business. It was stressful and exhausting. I wanted to relax for a while—I needed a break.

I was enjoying my new staff, a group of young people who were fun to work with. I'd spent quality, unrushed time with my boyfriend and dog.

For the first time since our move to River Grove, I wasn't stressed or fearful about who was after me.

Why would I want to do anything to mess that up?

Still, my mind had a mind of its own.

I couldn't stop it from thinking about the murder of Andrew Mehta. The shock of discovering his body—and then seeing my father's response to it. This morning, I'd tried to figure out how anyone, other than Reggie, could have gotten in to kill the champion. Could there have been some other way into the room? Something none of us were seeing?

I could tell from talking to my dad that he was heartbroken. He'd looked forward to this tournament for almost a year. He'd wanted to play a game with Andrew Mehta.

"I'm sure I'll be talking to the chief again," I said, seeing a hint of hope on his face. "If there's a way I can help, that doesn't interfere with my time at the bakery, maybe I can do it."

Just then I saw the kitchen door open. Chef Jorge rolled

out the case displaying Beck's cake, decorated in stark white and nearly black chocolate frosting that she'd made from black cocoa. There, on the top of the cake, a molded chocolate king piece lay toppled haphazardly across a single white chessboard square.

It was stark. High contrast.

It was clear what it meant.

Andrew Mehta should have been wrapping up his victory in the first River Grove Chess Tournament and moving on to a life of bigger victories and exciting possibilities.

Instead, he was being memorialized.

Chapter Twelve

Reggie and Beck came out of the kitchen to join us, as Chef Jorge wheeled the case into place by the lunch station.

"It's just right, Beck," Reggie said quietly to my assistant manager. "I appreciate you finishing it so quickly."

"It was easy, compared to the other cakes. Once I got the process down, each one went faster."

Reggie nodded, his expression kept hidden behind his sunglasses.

Beck and I got in the car and headed back to The Laughing Loaf, since I'd gotten a very passive-aggressive text message from Chloe asking if we were considering coming back anytime soon.

We saw the reason for Chloe's text for help as we pulled onto the road.

The line was out the door for The Laughing Loaf. Our big sun tea jug was on a stand near the door, probably filled with ice water. I took a glance at the temperature on my car —99 degrees.

Knowing how hot it was instantly made me feel worse.

Customers stood in line under the awning, chatting with each other as they sipped from cups. They looked relatively refreshed and not like they were succumbing to heatstroke. Whoever put the jug out front deserved five stars for customer service.

I parked the car in a spot on the street since it was easier than going down the alley to park.

"Looks like Rose and Chloe had everything under control," Beck said as we got out of the car. "Super smart putting out the water."

Chloe was at the front counter, along with Tyler and Evan, who were setting up for lunch.

We made our way in, trying to avoid people standing in line inside, who were just happy to be in the air conditioned space.

Chloe gave me a cheery look, though with gritted teeth. After going back to check on Biga and wash my hands, I came out and relieved her.

"We were gone less than an hour. What happened?" I looked out at the crowd as I took my place at the counter.

"The heat," she said, pulling her hair away from her sweaty face, twisting it and securing it on her head with a massive plastic clip. "We have better A/C here than they have at home. And everyone wants to talk about what happened last night. When Rose saw everyone in line looking hot and sweaty, she set out the ice water jug."

My newest baker was showing initiative. I'd take time to talk to her later. "Take a break, Chloe. I'll take over for a while."

Rose offered to continue running the espresso machine, since many customers wanted iced drinks.

"Salads and wraps are the thing today, apparently," Tyler said as he scooped salad mix into a bowl and covered it with chicken slices, garbanzo beans, cherry tomatoes, and croutons.

Soon Chloe brought up a tray of fresh flatbread to restock the lunch line. It smelled amazing. Now that she was back, Beck had taken over manning the oven, trying to keep up with the demand.

The dining area was packed, and the conversation was loud. Since it was Sunday, families had come in with kids. They ran around the tables and occasionally hid under them, leaving a trail of crayons and crumbs behind them. They were also noisy. *Very* noisy. Between the heat and the noise, I was getting a headache. I gulped water from my water bottle and rubbed my head.

At 1:00 p.m., when the line had died down, Mayor C came back for an extra-large Iced Café Americano.

"I'm wilting over at city hall, Gracie. Our only relief is a few old swamp coolers. You know, the old-school kind where you put water in them." The mayor fanned her face with a sheaf of papers. "I've got paperwork to finish for tomorrow morning. I'm having a hell of a time concentrating on it."

"Any news on the murder at The Riverside?"

The mayor shook her head. "Only that the crime scene team is there going over Mehta's room. The chief called me to tell me. He's betting on them finding something that helps with the case. He has no idea how to proceed with it otherwise."

"I can tell he's frustrated." I went to the display case and brought out an apple tart for her, on the house. "Corinne, I know you avoid it, but the sugar in this will help perk you right up."

"Why the hell not? It's going to kill us all anyway," the

mayor said gloomily, a look of resignation on her face. "Today I'm desperate."

With her "poisonous" treat in a bag, the mayor went to claim her americano at the pickup counter and head back to her office.

At two thirty, when the customers eating in the dining area had dwindled away, we closed the doors. From the back room, I heard Chloe scream, "Oh my God, it's finally over!"

Before we swept the messy floor of the dining area or cleaned up anything, I invited the staff up front. Elise and Daisy had just gotten back from The Riverside. After the two put the perishable items away in the fridge, they came and sat down with us.

"Iced drinks for everyone. Let's sit for a bit if you've got the time. If you have to go, no worries. You can take off."

"Hey, I have some leftovers from my cakes for Reggie and some chocolate pieces I didn't use. It was in the fridge, so it's cold, too." Beck brought out a plate with frosted cake chunks and a few random molded chess pieces.

We sat around the large table in the dining area, which I quickly discovered was covered with sticky handprints and spilled apple juice. Rose and I jumped up to get wet rags and wipe everything down.

We sat around the table for about twenty minutes, unloading about how crazy the day had been, but also talking about anything and everything.

Tyler, Evan, and Rose were curious about what had happened at The Riverside last night, since they'd heard customers talking about it today.

I told them as much as I could. I admitted that Reggie and I had found Andrew Mehta.

"It sounded like he was gasping for breath as we were

trying to get in," I said, describing how we finally got in when Reggie slid the chain lock open. "I called 911 right away but it was too late."

Evan asked, "How could somebody get in there to stab him if it was locked?"

"That's what the chief is trying to figure out," I said, slowly eating a piece of moist white cake with a fork. "Damn. This is good cake, Beck."

"It's one of my mom's favorite cake recipes," Beck said with a shy smile. "We had it for all our birthdays growing up."

"Why do you think he was killed, Gracie?" Rose asked with a thoughtful look on her face. "Did someone want to get him out of the tournament?"

"This is a very competitive group of players, but still—that seems like a stretch." The game itself was the obsession with most of the players I'd met. "This is a small tournament. It's not like there's a lot of money or prestige at stake."

"Maybe somebody at the tournament had a secret," Tyler speculated. "Andrew Mehta found out about it and was blackmailing them."

"All the players were talking about the murder at lunch at The Riverside today," Elise said, picking at her piece of cake. "Some of them said they're scared they could be next."

I'd been so focused on Andrew's death, I hadn't thought about that. If he was just the first, though, the killer would have to work fast—and do it today or possibly tomorrow during the community tournament.

A very unsettling thought.

Especially as I sat here enjoying some downtime with my staff.

I told my dad I'd do something to investigate if I had the time. But only a month ago, I'd been dodging Balkan dissidents who were hunting down one of my ex-husband's tech secrets. The tension from that time was slowly fading, but right now, what I wanted was a normal life. And a little bit of fun.

Daisy, who'd come back over with Elise after the lunch shift, was looking down at her plate, still laden with a piece of cake topped with chocolate buttercream. She had very curly blonde hair that she'd pulled back into a ponytail.

"How was your time at The Riverside today, Daisy?"

I asked, because she seemed a bit shy, not always knowing how to venture into the conversation.

She bit her lip and looked over at me.

"It was quiet today," she said softly, "compared to yesterday and Friday. Everyone's thinking about last night. They seem scared." She looked like she wanted to say something else.

"What else did you notice?" I asked gently.

"I recognized Andrew from his picture on the wall," she said, her voice growing quiet. Her face turned bright red. "He was really nice looking—"

Elise and Chloe nodded in enthusiastic agreement. "I always tried to smile at him—you know, to encourage him a little. Yesterday when he came through the lunch line, he looked unhappy. I asked him if he was okay." She dabbed at her eyes with a napkin. "He said no, he wasn't. That there was someone who was making life hard for him. They were pushing him to do something he didn't want to do."

Daisy took in a deep breath. "So all I could think of to say was: 'You should talk to Reggie. He might be able to help you.'" She shook her head, ashamed of her admission. "I just know Reggie is good at that."

Chloe nodded encouragingly. "Reggie *is* good at that. That was a good suggestion."

As Daisy told her story, I immediately thought of two things.

Younghee had seemed to play the role of the girlfriend who'd been cast aside in favor of chess. But what if she was more than that—maybe a stalker? Or at the least, someone who wouldn't leave him alone after their breakup last year.

I also thought of Reggie.

But maybe Andrew *had* confided in Reggie. And maybe Reggie had known more than he'd said last night. He hadn't shared anything with me about it. As I thought about Reggie's actions last night, I wondered. He'd seemed to have concerns about Andrew even before I'd approached him with what Younghee had said.

Maybe Reggie knew something. Of course, he could have already shared that with the chief. But I had a feeling he hadn't.

"I appreciate you sharing that, Daisy." I stood up, smiling at my staff who willingly stayed late to chat. "I should let you all go. Thanks for hanging in there on a very hot, very busy day. Great job, everyone. And Rose—thank you for putting the water jug out front for customers in line. Brilliant move."

Rose nodded. "It made sense with how hot it was."

As my staff dispersed and prepared to either go home or go to the back room to prep, I talked to Daisy as she pulled her water bottle out of the cold fridge.

"Daisy, would you be up for sharing what you just told us with the chief and Deputy Brad? It might make a difference to the case. They need all the info they can get right now."

Daisy looked a little frightened.

"The chief seems scary."

I tried not to laugh. "Yeah, he might come across a little

gruff. But he's a pretty nice guy. If you went in to tell him, he would be grateful to have the information. Trust me."

Daisy gave me a doubtful look. "So just go across the street to city hall? I guess I can do that."

After she left, I went into the back room and started in on prep for scones and cinnamon rolls.

I had some questions for Younghee Park.

And a few more for Reggie.

Chapter Thirteen

The cake break with the staff renewed my energy. It comforted me to have the staff together, chatting and sharing a little of themselves a month and a half into working together. We were getting to know each other, and I had a new appreciation for the quality of the people we'd hired.

Jeb knocked at the back door to pick Chloe up, looking embarrassed, since the two were only in the beginning stages of acknowledging their relationship to the River Grove public. Even though the town had figured it out long ago.

As Beck, Rose, and I busied ourselves with cleanup and some setup for bakes on Labor Day evening, the three of us continued with the sharing and camaraderie.

"Beck, I saw the cakes you made for the chess tourna-ment," Rose said as she wiped down the metal tables. "Amazing! They're so creative. I hope I can learn how to do that from you someday."

Beck went on to talk about how she'd grown up doing

decorations for her brothers' birthday cakes and now sometimes made cakes for her nieces' and nephews' birthdays.

"Maeve's birthday is next month. Wanna help me make her a cake?" Beck looked ecstatic at the prospect. "I want to make her something really special. Got any ideas?"

"Of course!"

Rose's face lit up. The two began talking about what might be a fitting theme for Maeve's cake. For several minutes, while they cleaned the back room, they went back and forth between all things Irish—maybe a Guinness chocolate cake—and a bread loaf lookalike that turned out to be a cake when you sliced into it.

I looked up at the clock in the backroom. It was 3:30 p.m. I had some prep to do but tomorrow was Labor Day. The Laughing Loaf would be closed, which meant I could really sleep in, and if I wanted to do a little fact-finding about Mehta and his murder, I'd have time to do it.

I'd also be able to go over to The Riverside for the community tournament, to support both my dad and Nate as they played. I could enjoy myself without having to rush back to The Laughing Loaf to work.

I felt my phone buzz in my apron pocket. I looked down and saw a text from Nate.

> You'll be free soon, right? No labor allowed on labor day.

> Want to do something tonight?

Nate must have finished the filing and cleanup in his studio.

> YES!

I'm going back to The Riverside tonight. R says you're welcome as my guest. Chef is grilling RIBS.

Nate immediately liked the text with a heart.

I'll come by to pick you up at 5:45

BECK AND ROSE left at 4:30 p.m., agreeing to come back for a prep session the next evening for Tuesday morning's opening.

I fed the gloppy starter in our starter tub, put in an order for flour and sugar on my computer, and did a final wipedown in the dining area. I was still finding crumbs from our cake break.

There was a tap on the front door. The chief stood outside, a grim look on his sweat-covered face.

I opened the door and waved him in.

"Dave, what's going on? What happened?"

His jaw was clenched tight. He looked down and shuffled his feet.

"I need to talk to you, Gracie. I'm on my way to The Riverside to arrest Reggie McFerrin."

Chapter Fourteen

I blinked.

"Chief. What's going on?" For a moment, I wondered if today's heat had gotten to him.

This made no sense.

I closed the door and invited him to the back room, where the A/C was pumping in lots of cool, fresh air.

I knew the chief didn't think the stools in our back room were legit seating, so I led him to my comfy executive chair. I pulled a bottled water from the fridge and handed it to him.

"Sit down and tell me what happened." I didn't have the time or energy to be polite.

I pulled up a stool and sat down across from him.

"Today I got a call from Mehta's coach. He's flying in tomorrow morning from San Diego. "His name's Sarkis Kaprelian."

"Okay." I wondered what this had to do with our investigation.

The chief pulled out a handkerchief and wiped the sweat off his forehead.

"When Kaprelian heard about a regional tournament in Northern California, he began thinking of a kid he'd played chess with when he was growing up in New England in the 1960s. He was a brilliant player, bound for a career in chess at a world champion level. His parents were rich, and the kid grew up knowing he'd have to give up chess because he was expected to take over the family business—his father was a banker. He owned one of the biggest banks on the East Coast.

"But the late 1960s was a time of anti-war protests and young people turning against the values of their parents. Hippies. Kaprelian told me his chess-playing friend rebelled against the lifestyle he'd grown up in. He hated the pressure his parents put on him to take over the banking business, which he had no interest in.

"Sarkis said his friend also began to resent the pressure he put on himself to win at chess, so he quit chess. Quit everything. He lived on the streets for a while. Started hanging around with musicians. He moved into a commune in upstate New York. One day, he completely disappeared —along with $750,000 of his parents' money."

The chief handed me a printout of a missing persons report, dated July, 1969.

There was a blurry photo of a young man with long dark hair and a moustache, along with details of the man's background, as reported by his parents. The missing man's name was Leonard Reginald Fortiner.

The face was thinner and smoother, but I recognized it right away.

My heart was pounding. This was Reggie.

"His parents and friends never heard from him again. Some say he moved out to San Francisco and died of a drug overdose. But he'd stopped living under the name Leonard Reginald Fortiner. He took a new name."

I nodded and tried to picture this young Reggie. What he must have been feeling. How comfortable he must have felt, surrounded by musicians instead of bankers.

"Over the years, Kaprelian did some research and suspected that this old friend from his chess days was now calling himself Reggie McFerrin and owned a music venue in the California redwoods." The chief wiped his forehead again and paused to open the bottle of water. He took a huge gulp. "So, when the tournament came up in the listings with the location of The Riverside Saloon, Kaprelian asked his protégé Andrew Mehta to register for it. He shared the story with Mehta and told him to ask Reggie if it was true." The chief took another drink. "Kaprelian admitted he may have put a little too much pressure on Mehta to do this."

I slumped on the stool. "So you think Mehta brought it up to Reggie. And that Reggie actually killed him for it?"

The chief lay back against the chair and rubbed his eyes for a moment. He had a pasty, worn-out look to him today. I wondered how much sleep he'd gotten over the past two days.

He turned to me, frowning.

"Gracie, we've got a crime where one person, only one person, had access to the victim's room. Reggie was the only one who had the room keys," he said, his tone dull. "He knew how to get past the chain lock."

I shook my head. "This doesn't make any sense. I get that Reggie could have stolen money from his parents and run away sixty years ago. I can believe that. But I can't imagine Reggie killing someone."

The chief looked at me with heavy-lidded eyes and tightened his lips.

"Gracie, it's not just the access to the room. Today the crime scene team found Reggie's fingerprints on the nightstand, on Mehta's phone, and on a champagne glass on the stand. They're checking the glass for DNA right now."

I thought back to those tense minutes when Reggie and I went into the room and saw Mehta's body. And when I was calling 911. Had Reggie picked up Mehta's things? Had he brought his glass into the room when he came in— or had it been there when we came in? I didn't remember that he'd had a glass with him when we came in.

"First of all, Reggie's fingerprints could have been all over the nightstand and everywhere else in the room," I said, defensively. "That would be normal. He *owns* the place."

"Gracie, we've got two things on Reggie—or Leonard Fortiner—right now. He was the only one with access to Mehta's room. And he had a big secret to hide. Mehta probably confronted him with that, since Kaprelian asked him to. I'm sorry to say it since I like Reggie." The chief's face twisted as he said it. "He's been a big part of this town for sixty years. He's been mayor four times."

My mind raced as I tried to think of what to do here. The chief was ready to go over to The Riverside and arrest the director of the first River Grove Chess Tournament, while the players, still reeling from the murder of one of their own, finished their final games.

This was going to hit my dad hard.

"Let me talk to Reggie first." I stood up. My mind was still absorbing the news about Reggie not being Reggie but a man on the run with a secret to hide. It didn't entirely surprise me, but given the circumstances, he owed us an explanation. "It's only fair to hear his side of the story."

The chief grunted and shook his head. "Gracie, this is a police matter. What makes you think you can call the shots here? You wouldn't know about this unless I'd told you—"

"Yeah, but *why* did you stop here to tell me? You didn't go directly to The Riverside and arrest him yourself," I blurted out with anger and a little bit of desperation. "Admit it. You didn't think it was the right thing to do either."

The chief let out a weary sigh and stood up. "Fine. Let's go."

I took my apron off and threw it in the dirty apron bin, and I grabbed my purse. Then I remembered. Biga was still in his pen in the other room.

"I have to take Biga with us."

The chief groaned. "Oh, for crying out loud, Gracie. He's just a damned dog."

"I am not leaving him here." I stood my ground. "Not by himself."

"Bring him, then, for all I care." The chief rolled his eyes. He stood there, arms crossed against his chest, his foot tapping impatiently.

I went into Biga's pen and got him into the crate. Completely unaware of the situation, he was excited to be getting out of dog jail. His tail wagged excitedly.

We headed out the back door of the bakery, and I locked the door behind us.

After I slid into the passenger seat of the squad car, I quickly texted Nate, since I'd made plans to meet with him.

Change of plans

> Something big happened. Meet me at
> Riverside at 6:30. I'll tell you then.

The chief pulled up to the parking lot at The Riverside. Thankfully he did this quietly and without the blare of a siren and lights.

When we walked in, I noticed more action at The Riverside than there had been this morning. The staff was preparing for dinner, the downstairs had been rearranged, and the dividers and lunch area had been taken down.

I felt like I had a lump of lead in my stomach. I dreaded this conversation with Reggie. But I also wanted to know. Part of this did not surprise me. Reggie was a mystery to me when I met him. He always wore sunglasses so no one ever saw his eyes. Who was he and why had he come here? I wanted to know the whole story.

And I wanted to hear it from him.

Following the chief, I carried Biga's crate through the doors of The Riverside.

"Just a sec, chief. I'm going to see if I can put Biga in the utility room."

The chief scowled as he waited.

I opened the door of the room and saw the same setup from the other night. I released Biga into the gated space and left him with a treat, feeling like a neglectful parent.

I didn't see Reggie downstairs. I approached Drake at the bar, where a few players sat hunched over their drinks. The bartender smiled at me, but when he saw the chief behind me, he stiffened. I wondered if he suspected something was going on.

"Is Reggie around?" I asked.

"He's upstairs in his office, making a phone call." Drake

shot a suspicious look at the chief. "I can let him know you're on your way up."

"If you could," I said, trying to smile but failing. I wanted to cry. I wanted to yell at somebody, but this wasn't the chief's fault. I hoped our conversation upstairs wouldn't end in Reggie's arrest.

"Thanks, Drake."

The chief and I made our way to the stairs. I looked out the windows at the San Luciano River below, sparkling in the late afternoon sunlight. I wished I were there, walking along the riverbank and skipping rocks with Nate. Not heading upstairs to confront a good friend about his past.

We walked into the lounge outside Reggie's office. The chief put a hand on my arm and kept his voice low as he spoke.

"I was planning on letting you introduce this, but now I'm thinking I should take the lead here."

It made sense, though the thought of hearing what he'd say and seeing Reggie's reaction made me feel sick to my stomach.

I tapped lightly on Reggie's door, which was ajar.

"Come in, Gracie," Reggie called, then added, "and Dave." I pushed open the door and Reggie waved us in. I made sure I closed the door behind us.

"Please have a seat." His voice was steady, though his face was so drained of color he really did resemble a vampire. Did he know what we were here to talk about?

He leaned forward in his purple leather executive chair and set his elbows on the desk expectantly.

"Reggie, I received a call from Sarkis Kaprelian, a chess coach who worked with Andrew Mehta. He also said he was in your chess club when you were a teenager back in Connecticut, in the 1960s."

If Reggie was surprised, his face didn't show it.

"I know Sarkis."

"He is flying up from San Diego. He wants to meet with you."

The chief continued with the story Sarkis had told him about the disappearance of his friend Leonard Reginald Fortiner—only son of a wealthy banking family and an up-and-coming chess player in New England tournaments. And how he'd drained $750,000 from one of his father's accounts. And how, in June of 1969, he disappeared completely, with no word to his parents or friends.

"Reggie, I need you to confirm for me." The chief's voice sounded hoarse. "Are you Leonard Fortiner?"

The room was still. I didn't even hear sounds filtering up from downstairs. No clinking glasses at the bar. No voices. Just silence.

As if everyone at The Riverside had paused for his answer.

The chief's question hung in the air.

"I am," Reggie said quietly.

The chief seemed caught off guard, as if he'd expected Reggie to deny it.

"Then I need to ask you some questions." The chief pulled out his tablet and turned it on. "Did Andrew Mehta approach you and ask you about your former identity and your disappearance?"

Reggie folded his hands in front of him.

"He did. He told me Sarkis pressured him to ask me. I knew Andrew was going to take that information back to Sarkis. And that Sarkis would make it public."

"When did you tell Mehta the truth about your past?" The chief's fingers were poised over his tablet ready for his answer.

"Yesterday afternoon." Reggie wove his fingers together. "For almost sixty years, I've lived a very different life. Before I talked to Mehta, I had to figure out how to explain my actions when I was nineteen. I was busy all day with the tournament yesterday. Finally, after his last match, I asked Mehta to meet me here. I told him everything."

The chief sat up in his chair and gave Reggie a straight-on look.

"Reggie—or uh, Leonard—did you kill Andrew Mehta to keep him from revealing your secret?"

Reggie did something unusual. He took off his sunglasses, something I'd only seen him do once. The last time had been when we'd discovered Andrew dead in his room.

After seeing him in his aviator sunglasses for so long, I was startled at how small Reggie's eyes seemed. They were surrounded by swirls of wrinkles, almost like the apertures on a camera. He left his sunglasses off for the rest of our meeting.

"I did not kill him. I hadn't seen him since our talk. When I went upstairs with Gracie to get into his room, I was devastated at what I saw." He winced now as he thought about it.

"Yet you were the only one who had keys to the room," the chief said pointedly. "And you were able to take that chain lock off easily."

Reggie nodded soberly. "I can only tell you the truth, Dave. I did not kill Andrew Mehta. If anything, I knew what it was like to be in his position because that used to be *me*. I was a chess champion myself. I held on to that identity till it started to kill me. I talked to him about the supplements and the drugs he'd been taking. I asked him if he felt trapped."

The chief didn't seem to know what to say to this. He shook his head and lifted his hands helplessly. "I don't even know what that means, Reggie. How can I help you? You were the only one besides Mehta with access to that room. And you had a motive—to keep him from telling the world who you are and what you did sixty years ago."

Reggie looked down at his hands.

"I'm not proud of everything I've done. I didn't think I could hide forever. It's time to face my past. Mehta gave me a gift by confronting me."

The chief looked frustrated. He looked down at his tablet. Then up at Reggie. This wasn't easy. He wanted cut-and-dried, and he was not getting it.

"Reggie, there's no other set of room keys here? Would housekeeping have another set for the cleaners?" I asked. He shook his head.

I was starting to feel desperate. "Not even a set of keys from when The Riverside was your commune?"

Reggie smiled softly, as if a fond memory of those days was replaying in his head. "No, the locks were replaced when we remodeled. The guests and I have the only copies of the keys."

"Reggie, listen to me," the chief said firmly, clinging to the reason he was here. "You own this place. Is it possible that anybody else could have gotten into Mehta's room before you opened that door last night?"

Reggie knotted his fingers together and raised his head to look the chief in the eye.

"I can't see any way that could happen," he said matter-of-factly.

The chief unsnapped a pair of handcuffs from his belt and stood up.

"Then Reggie—*uh*, Leonard Reginald Fortiner—I'm arresting you for the murder of Andrew Mehta."

Chapter Fifteen

The chief had delayed so long, I didn't think he'd actually do it.

"What good would it do to arrest Reggie? He's not going to run away. He's in the middle of running a chess tournament."

Reggie nodded tiredly. "She's right." He took the big ring of keys from his pocket and laid them down on the desk in front of us.

I thought quickly.

"If Reggie says he didn't do it, I believe him."

An idea was forming in my head, and I wondered if the killer had intended to implicate Reggie—with no other way to get into the room but the saloon owner's keys.

"Think about this. If word gets out that you're still looking for Mehta's killer, the real killer could get nervous and try to leave town. If you announce that you've arrested someone—Reggie—for the murder, then the killer will relax, maybe stick around for the rest of the tournament. They might feel smart, a little cocky, that they've gotten away with it. And they might slip up."

The chief gave me one of his glares, which meant: "You came up with an idea I didn't think of. How *dare* you."

The case was confounding him, and I suspected he hadn't felt at all in control since that 911 call last night. I don't think he believed Reggie killed Mehta, but he also didn't see how anyone else at the tournament could have done it.

"Gracie has a point," Reggie said calmly, tilting his head, as if I'd recommended a nice place to have dinner, not suggested that he be arrested. "If you make the killer feel comfortable, he or she will relax. Maybe a little too much. I think it's worth a try." Reggie looked up expectantly at the chief.

"So, tell me, Dave. What can I do to help?"

The chief eyed Reggie with a look of puzzlement, as the handcuffs dangled from his hand. I tried to imagine what he was thinking. Much as I respected the chief, he was pretty easy to read. He stood awkwardly for a moment, shaking his head.

"You *want* me to arrest you."

Reggie nodded at the chief. "It makes sense to do it. The only problem is that John Markley will have to take over my duties for the rest of the tournament. I don't think he's prepared for that. There's a lot I do with the food and accommodations at The Riverside, besides the tournament. Willow Barrett, my housekeeping manager, can handle some of that."

"The bakery's closed tomorrow," I said, preferring to focus on logistics than the reality of Reggie being arrested for murder. "I can be here if you need me for help with the food and the guest services. If that's taken care of, my dad could probably handle the chess side of things."

The chief looked at Reggie, then over at me, completely

befuddled at this point. "So I'm going to arrest you, Reggie." He read the saloon owner his rights, then Reggie stood up and cheerfully presented his wrists for the handcuffs.

The chief snapped the cuffs on, then put his hand on Reggie's back, ready to walk him downstairs. This felt surreal. My kind, quirky friend, who regularly meditated in the woods and was my dog's best friend, was being arrested for murder.

"Wait, let's talk about this," I said, trying to think this through. "It's 6:30 p.m. When will people start gathering for dinner, Reggie?"

"In about ten minutes." He looked up at the old bar clock on his wall. "I'd give it twenty if you want a full crowd at the table, Dave."

I looked down at my phone and saw a message from Nate.

> Where are you?

I quickly texted back:

> Upstairs. We're coming down. It will not be what it looks like. Please tell my dad that.

"Fine," the chief sighed, clearly uncomfortable with this. "In fifteen minutes, we'll go downstairs and to the squad car. We'll process you in my office at city hall. We'll determine the next step there." He looked at Reggie uncertainly, almost as if asking for his approval or for a sudden confession.

"Give me just a few minutes," Reggie said, looking at his phone, which he couldn't really pick up, being in handcuffs. "We should be good. I need to ping my housekeeping manager Willow and leave messages for John

Markley and Jorge. Gracie, can you hold my phone for me?"

I held the phone up to him, while he used his voice to send his texts. Once he'd finished, I started thinking about how Reggie's arrest could make the biggest impact on the guests downstairs.

"We need to make sure people see Reggie coming down the stairs—so everyone knows he is being arrested."

Reggie brightened. "I was arrested at protests in Chicago in the '60s. I've got this."

At 6:25 p.m., the chief, looking triumphant—and a little confused—stood behind a handcuffed Reggie and shepherded him down the front stairs into the main room of The Riverside.

The room was crowded and starting to get noisy. When they heard loud steps on the stairs, they looked up in shock as we came down. The room fell silent.

Reggie played it up. "Stop this! You have no right to do this to me." He squirmed hammily in front of the chief, as if he were trying to ease his hands out of the cuffs. "I'm an old man. These cuffs are hurting me. This is police brutality!"

We walked past the crowd, which had stood up when they'd seen us come down. The noise level rose as everyone realized they were seeing the River Grove Chess Tournament director—and a pillar of the River Grove community —being arrested and led away by the police.

It was hard watching people's faces, since no one else but us knew what was happening. The players and their significant others sat dumbstruck, frozen in place. The dinner staff in their whites came out of the kitchen and stood against the wall, watching, two of them in tears. Chef Jorge came through the kitchen doors and watched Reggie coming down the stairs, a look of anguish on his face.

I looked for my dad in the crowd and found him— standing at the end of the dining table, his eyes riveted on Reggie as we walked him to the main door. My dad was even paler than usual, and there was hurt, not shock, in his eyes. I felt his pain like a stab in my heart: Did he think his friend had murdered Andrew Mehta? That, after all their time planning this tournament, his close friend was not who he'd appeared to be?

Then I saw Nate. Standing near the double doors. We passed him as we walked with Reggie to the parking lot.

I didn't know what to say, what look to give him.

Nate didn't nod. He looked at the three of us then frowned and turned away as if what he'd seen made no sense to him.

I pushed open the double doors and Reggie, the chief, and I headed for the squad car in the orange glow of the setting sun.

Chapter Sixteen

The chief drove around to the back of city hall. We parked, then I got out and the chief released Reggie from the squad car's caged back seat.

As we walked in the back entrance, Mayor C was at the door, on her way out.

She noticed Reggie in the handcuffs, then the chief, then me.

"What is going on here?" She stopped with the door half open, ready to lay into the chief. "What the hell have you done, Dave? *Tell me.*" Her eyes were fierce, her face red with anger.

Last year, under pressure from the local press, the chief had arrested someone for a murder, someone who clearly hadn't committed the crime. It caused a huge rift between the mayor and the chief. By the look on the mayor's face, she thought this was happening again.

"Corinne, do you have a few minutes?" I asked as the chief herded Reggie toward his office down the hall. The chief turned and flashed me a grateful look.

We headed down the hall to her office, which she'd just left. She flicked on her lights, and we sat down.

"Tell me what's happening, Gracie. This isn't looking good."

"Let me explain," I said once I caught my breath. "It's a lot, so here goes."

I told her about the call the chief had had with chess coach Sarkis Kaprelian, and the story of Reggie's running away in 1969, amid the pressures of being a local chess champion and heir to his father's bank.

Then I told him about Mehta confronting Reggie about his identity, at the request of his coach.

"I'm not sure whether the chief thinks Reggie actually killed Mehta. I don't think he does. Still, it's hard to see any other way the murder could have happened." Then I told her about my suggestion, backed by Reggie, that the chief arrest Reggie in front of the dinner guests—to put the real killer at ease enough to get overconfident and sloppy.

The mayor sat back in her chair and rubbed her forehead.

"So Reggie isn't really Reggie after all." She raised her eyebrows and sighed. "I'm not surprised. He seems the most likely person I know to have a mysterious backstory."

It wasn't a laughable situation, but I laughed nervously, because it was so true. If I'd ever suspected Reggie had a hidden past, I now knew for sure. I had so many questions I wanted answers to.

"I'll have to talk to the chief," Mayor C said, still deep in thought. "Do you know what he intends to do? He's not going to book Reggie—or Leonard—into the county jail, is he?" Then she rubbed her head, her eyes wide and bleary. She threw her head back. "Dear God. There's a storage closet we use for a town holding cell. We've only used it for

DUIs. This was part of River Grove's rebellion against being folded into Santa Cruz County's jurisdiction. Dave may want to use it for Reggie."

This was something I'd never heard of. Another River Grove secret revealed. "Can I see the cell?"

Mayor C set down her backpack and slid it under her desk. She opened her desk drawer and pulled out a rusty key with a tag attached to it. "The chief let me store some things in it for the chili cookoff in June."

She didn't have to show me, but I was intrigued now. I followed her down the hallway, till we turned the corner to a hall that ended in a big door with several layers of paint on it from years of changes. River Grove City Hall used to be Meyers Hardware, established in 1922. In the 1990s, when the store went out of business, it became the new city hall.

Mayor C inserted the key into the lock and turned, but the door stuck. She pushed her shoulder against it, and the door opened to reveal a windowless storage space with wood plank flooring. Ancient-looking shelves held wooden crates with faded old-timey fruit labels. A battered captain's chair sat on one side near the door, and in the middle of the room stood a cot with a wrought-iron bedframe, made up with sheets and a comforter. The place felt like a time capsule; it smelled musty, like old office supplies or a library.

"It's what we've got," the mayor said with a sigh, which wasn't the first time I'd heard that explanation given for River Grove facilities. "If I know anything about Reggie—or *Leonard*—it's that he'd rather stay in River Grove than be booked into Santa Cruz's facilities."

"I agree." I put my hand down on the cot mattress, which had as much give as a marble countertop.

"I'll put in a word," she said with a shrug. "And I will

trust that the chief does his usual and resists anything that involves the county."

"You have more power than you know, Corinne."

We walked back to her office, while she asked me more clarifying questions about Reggie's arrest.

The events of the day were starting to hit me hard. I needed to get back to The Riverside. I was hoping that Reggie's very public arrest would have an effect on the killer.

Failing that, I'd figure out how to stage a jailbreak.

"We both know how by-the-book the chief is, so he'll probably go through with it and book him here or in Santa Cruz," I said, remembering the conflicted look on the chief's face. "Reggie's fully on board with this plan, especially if it brings Mehta's killer out into the open."

Mayor C shook her head and peered down the hall in the direction of the chief's office. "This is ridiculous. Gracie, can you believe for one second that Reggie killed this chess player?"

"Nope. But I don't know who the real killer is either."

"Reggie shouldn't do jail time. He's what—eighty years old?"

I looked down at my phone. I needed to get back to the dinner banquet. If the killer was to reveal themself, it could be tonight. "Actually, if Reggie was nineteen years old when he disappeared in 1969, he's seventy-five now."

The mayor frowned. "Huh. I would have thought he was older. Still, there's no way he belongs in a jail cell. I'm going to talk to the chief."

Chapter Seventeen

As the mayor headed to the chief's office, I walked back to The Riverside. At 7:00 p.m., with the sun disappearing, it had cooled off. A soft breeze blew through town.

If there was a time for me to stop hiding in my happy little personal bubble, it was now. I needed to find the person responsible for Andrew Mehta's death. Reggie would probably be okay, even if the killer didn't make himself known tonight, but he'd be in for a prolonged legal battle.

It was the last night before the players and their significant others left the tournament to go home.

I walked through the main doors of The Riverside to see everyone gathered at the table, starting in on the baby back ribs Chef Jorge had grilled. I scanned the table and found Nate, who was sitting next to my dad. Nate had saved me a seat next to him.

I wore jeans and a t-shirt dusted with flour and little globs of dough, so I wasn't exactly dressed for a nice dinner. I pulled my chair out and sat down anyway.

Nate reached for my hand under the table.

He leaned toward me and whispered.

"Reggie's okay?"

"Yes. The chief came over to arrest him because there's been a new development." I kept my voice low. "It doesn't mean Reggie did it, but it's big news. When we get a chance to get away, I'll tell you the whole story."

Nate sighed and looked around the table. He was probably thinking the same as I was—the killer was sitting somewhere at this table.

"So the chief coming down the stairs with Reggie was just for show?"

I nodded. "For the most part. And that whole 'get your hands off me, copper,' act of Reggie's."

Nate smiled for the first time tonight.

"Yeah," he said. "That's when I figured out this wasn't what it looked like."

I leaned toward the table and my eyes met the eyes of my dad, who was on the other side of Nate.

"Hey, dad. Wanna go with me to the storage room to see Biga? I think he's lonely."

My dad had been keeping to himself, looking gloomy and lost in thought. "What? Right now?"

I nodded. "We need to go see Biga. *Now*."

"But surely with everything going on—" he started in.

Nate put a hand on his shoulder and said quietly and firmly, "Your daughter needs to tell you something, John."

My dad and I stood up and headed toward the storage room outside the kitchen doors.

When I opened the door, our little furball popped up from where he was curled up on the floor.

"Biga boy!" I opened the gate and sat down with him on

the floor. He jumped into my lap excitedly and began burrowing into my arms.

"Reggie sent me a text." My dad pulled up a folding chair and sat down next to us. "He said something came up and I needed to handle the rest of the tournament by myself. He says he'll explain everything later and not to worry. He didn't tell me he was going to be arrested. Everyone at dinner said he was arrested for Andrew's murder. That can't be true."

I told him about the arrest, but it was Reggie's place, not mine, to reveal his identity. I told him the chief had been unable to get past the fact that Reggie was the only one able to access Mehta's room. He had to make an arrest—but I thought that might draw the real killer out into the open. And Reggie had gone along with the plan.

"Perhaps it will draw the killer out," my father said, clenching his hands together tightly. "But what if it doesn't? What happens to Reggie then?"

"I'm going to do what I can tonight to speed things up with the investigation. Dad, I think you know I haven't wanted to. I was hoping the chief and Brad would take care of this. My life is good right now, really good. I've been stressed for so long. Now I'm not." I rubbed a stray tear off my face. "But since yesterday I've been thinking about things I noticed. Things I heard when I was talking to the players last night. I have to do something now. Reggie's not the one who should be in jail."

My dad looked at me directly, his brow furrowed. "What came up that made the chief want to arrest him tonight?"

"I know something about that, but Reggie would want to explain it to you himself. You two are friends. Whatever you hear about him after this, Reggie's a good person, and we both know that."

My father blinked. He was processing some intense things, and his normally reserved exterior showed it. He leaned over in his chair to pet Biga, who was sniffing at him and licking his hands. He must have been smelling the baby back ribs on him, the little scrounge.

"Dad, if you're in charge of the tournament now, it might be a good idea to go out there and say something to the group. They're probably confused, and they're already dealing with the loss of Mehta. You are still doing the final matches tomorrow—and the community games—right?"

My father nodded, then spoke with a new firmness in his voice. "We could cancel it. But I don't want to. Reggie and I planned this, and we wanted it to be a time to celebrate the game. I am not going to send players home on this note."

"Go out there and tell them." I scratched Biga's head as he curled into my lap. "Reggie told me something on Friday. He said you gave him his enthusiasm back for chess. He remembered how much he used to love the game when he was younger. That came back to him every time you played chess together."

"He said that?" My dad raised his eyebrows and smiled faintly.

With a few more cuddles for Biga and reassurances that I'd be back later to free him from his utility room confinement, my dad and I went back to dinner.

As I walked back to the table, I thought about the funny coincidence.

Reggie had a secret identity. And he'd had it decades before my dad and I had entered witness protection.

The difference was, he'd chosen it for himself.

Chapter Eighteen

My dad, with his best friend having just been arrested, gave a stirring speech to the people assembled at the dinner table.

"You came to our small town to play chess together. All of us love the game. Andrew Mehta lived for the game. Reggie, whom you saw taken away, loves chess. He and I planned this event to bring the best of the West Coast players together in one place. And despite all that has happened, this has been an exciting tournament, and the level of play has been excellent."

A few people clapped, but many people sat dully, stunned by the events of the past two days. They weren't even talking to each other, just sitting there sipping the last of their drinks. Younghee's face looked pale and distressed as she took a sip from her wine glass. Patrick slumped in his seat, his eyes shifting around the room, looking defensive. Derek and Kendra Bartolo were reunited, but they looked like they wanted to be anywhere but here. Trey Godwin was fraying the edges of his napkin into fringe. I scanned the table, trying to spot anyone who looked relieved or happy after Reggie's arrest.

"I ask you now," my dad said, his eyes watery. He was showing a passion I had rarely seen in him. "See this tournament through. We have one more day—for our fourth round of tournament play. Then we'll have a time for players from the community to come in and play. Since we are here in this beautiful place for a little while longer, I ask you—let's make the best of this time and enjoy the game we love."

"But what about Mehta?" someone called out from the end of the table. "Does this mean Reggie was the killer?"

My father kept his composure, though I could see how hard it was for him to say these words. "I must tell you it appears to be true. Reggie was arrested based on evidence found by the police."

Conversations erupted as the group processed this.

"How can you say that we are safe after what has happened?" Maya Singh's mother spoke up from the end of the table. "My young daughter is here. How do I know she won't be harmed?"

"The police are maintaining a presence here at The Riverside. Police Chief Westerman assured me that Mehta alone was targeted and that there appears no need for the rest of us to fear."

There were murmurs of relief around the table.

"Obviously, our pairings for the fourth round have changed. But these will be exciting games indeed, and I look forward to watching with you from the skittles area. Then we'll open the doors to the River Grove community for games. You're more than welcome to participate in these as well."

My dad reached down to pick up a glass of water and take a gulp. His energy was dipping, I could see. This was incredibly hard for him, right after witnessing his friend being taken away.

"Once again, thank you for your patience during this time. I appreciate the energy, excitement, and skill you've all brought to this tournament. The kitchen staff will clear the table at 9:00 p.m., but feel free to stay as long as you want."

With that, he returned to his seat next to me. A few people clapped. I put my arms around him and hugged him. I was so proud of him.

"That must have been hard, dad. Reggie would be proud."

Nate reached over and touched his arm. "Well done, John," he whispered.

My dad nodded and wiped his eyes, which were tearing up.

I wanted more than this tonight. I wanted someone to stand up, moved by my dad's speech, and confess to Andrew's murder. It didn't look like that was going to happen.

That's when it became clear to me. If anything was going to change this situation and get Reggie released, *I* was going to have to make it happen.

I went back to the utility room where Biga was waiting and pulled out my wallet. I searched for the business card of Willow Barrett, The Riverside's housekeeping manager. She'd left before dinner tonight.

I needed her help. And a place to stay tonight.

I took out my phone to call and saw that I had a text from my friend, Elana.

Reggie's been arrested?

This can't be true! Call me!

I didn't want to tell the story one more time.

It's true, E. I can't talk right now.

Meet up next week for drinks?

I typed in Willow's number and waited. It was 8:45 p.m., and I was hoping it wasn't too late to call. I remembered my proper mother telling me when I was a teenager: "A lady never calls before 9:00 a.m. or after 9:00 p.m."

I was good, then.

"Willow, this is Gracie Markley. I'm at The Riverside."

Willow's reply sounded hoarse and like she didn't really want to talk. "If this is about Reggie, I've heard everything. Jorge called me."

"I'm figuring out some things here that might get Reggie released. But I need some help. I need a room here for tonight. And a list of who's in what room."

Willow sighed heavily. "Yeah, well, let me see if I can get that to you. I mean, it's totally against our rules. But Reggie told me that you figure out things the police can't. It's worth taking a chance if it helps Reggie. I'll text you a list."

"Thank you, Willow," I said. "And it would help if I could talk to any of the crew who were working here last night during dinner."

There was a shuffling noise, then a *thunk*, as if Willow had dropped the phone. Half a minute later, I heard her voice.

"Sorry about that. I've got something for you—there's a room available next to Reggie's office. It's small and not fancy. It's where we put overflow musicians or concertgoers who are too drunk to drive home. We also store our house guitars in there, so it's a little cluttered. You have Reggie's keys?"

"They're in his office."

"Then the room's yours. So you want to know about last night. We had a housekeeper doing his rounds—Kimo. Big dude from Hawaii. You can talk to him. He's on till eleven. And the kitchen staff can help you—that would be Francisco and Marisol."

"Thank you, Willow. I appreciate it."

I hung up and went back to the dinner table. Most of the guests had gone to their rooms, and the busboys were clearing the table. Nate and my dad had reconvened at the bar, where they sat talking soberly.

"I'm going to stay here tonight," I announced to them. "I've got a few things to work through. And I need to talk to the night housekeeper and the kitchen crew about last night."

The look on my father's face surprised me. The sad, lusterless look faded and his eyes had new focus. It was like in JRR Tolkien's *The Two Towers* when the slimy advisor, Wormtongue, loses his hold on King Théoden's mind. The king's stupor melts away and he returns to clarity. There was a look of hope in my dad's eyes.

"You're going to figure it out, aren't you, dear?"

Nate stood up, a worried look on his face. "Gracie, the killer is staying here tonight, too."

He swallowed, and then his look softened. I saw his lip tremble.

"Trust me. Please," I said softly in his ear.

He nodded, then came over and wrapped his arms around me. "You know I do."

"I'll keep the phone next to me," I said, resting my head

on his chest. "Please give dad and Biga a ride home. Biga's crate is with him in the utility room."

I left him with a kiss and headed for the back stairs.

To Reggie's office and my cell for the night.

Chapter Nineteen

R eggie's keys were still on his desk, where they'd been since his arrest. I picked up the iron ring, which was heavier than it looked.

I looked around Reggie's office, taking in this room that I'd been in so many times before. His patchouli and sandalwood scent still hung in the air.

There sat his comfy purple leather chair, vintage paisley wallpaper on the walls, and the thick indigo carpet. On the wall hung posters of bands of all genres from the past sixty years, signed by the musicians themselves. Led Zeppelin, Jimi Hendrix, the funk group Parliament, The Grateful Dead, Bob Marley, and the Foo Fighters. It was eclectic and very Reggie.

Mr. and Mrs. Fortiner, how could you possibly think your son was born to be a banker?

I hated to be a snoop, but I was. So I opened drawers and started looking around.

A large drawer on the lefthand side of the desk contained a big stack of file folders, labeled for receipts, musician contacts, and Riverside employee contacts.

Underneath these was an old-fashioned, leather-bound ledger, which looked like it was for The Riverside accounting records. It was more Reggie's style to maintain something handwritten, but The Riverside was a large and profitable operation. Records were probably digital and in the hands of an accounting firm.

I opened it, just to see.

A stack of papers fell out. Handwritten letters on stationery, printed emails, and a couple of newspaper clippings, yellowed and fragile.

A letter written in an elegant, spidery handwriting was from Louise Fortiner, dated June 11, 1970.

> *Dearest Leonard,*
>
> *Today is your birthday. I don't even know if you are alive. I certainly do not care about the money. Some say you are in San Francisco, where all the young people seem to be right now.*
>
> *I miss you with all my heart. I know you think of your father and I as one, but that is not true.*
>
> *He's hurt you with his anger, in every way you can hurt a person, trying to bend you to his will. You may never choose to see me again because of that, but I want you to know that I have loved you and seen that spark in you that makes you who you are.*
>
> *My dear, never, ever let it go out.*
>
> *With love from your mother,*
> *Louise Sprague Fortiner*

My throat constricted with tears. This was what Reggie ran away from. I grieved for him, and at the same time I felt bad for reading something so private.

That didn't stop me from continuing to shuffle through the pile, however.

There was a newspaper clipping from that same year, from *The Hartford Courant.*

Leonard Fortiner to Head to World Chess Finals in Moscow

IT FEATURED a photo of Reggie as an eighteen-year-old, with very short black hair. He was holding a trophy, surrounded by men in black suits, skinny ties, and glasses.

Another clipping showed the photo from the missing persons report that the chief had shown me. Reggie with long, scraggly hair, a grim look on his face.

No Sign of Fortiner Heir After Six Months: 750K Still Unaccounted For

If there was a time in history for someone like Reggie to disappear, 1969 was as good as any. The country was in upheaval, and young adults were protesting and cutting ties with their parents.

He disappeared in February of that year, so it looked like Reggie never did make it to the world championships, which would have started in April.

Reggie had abruptly turned his back on chess.

Another thing I found in the stack was an email from 1999. It was from Sarkis Kaprelian, who would go on to be Mehta's coach.

Mr. McFerrin

I am looking for a friend of mine, Leonard Fortiner, who disappeared in 1969.

My research shows that you arrived in California in 1969 and eventually started an inn in the Santa Cruz mountains. I've tracked down a photo of the inn's owner. It bears a strong resemblance to my friend.

If you are Leonard, please respond to this email. If you are not, please accept my apologies for wasting your time.

Sarkis Kaprelian
Coach and Owner
La Jolla Chess Academy

Five years later, Kaprelian sent a follow-up email, asking the same questions. I wondered why Reggie kept the correspondence. I suspected that he had not gotten back to Mehta's coach, and that had been the reason Kaprelian had pushed Mehta to confront Reggie at the tournament.

I picked up all the papers and put them back in the ledger, feeling like an intruder. Reggie was a private person, and I had rooted through information that he might never have chosen to show me or anyone else.

I wondered if he had ever contacted his mother. I hoped he had.

I glanced at my phone. It was 9:30 p.m. Kimo, the night housekeeper, was on duty till 11.

First things first.

I needed to talk to the kitchen staff, who were almost done cleaning up.

I grabbed Reggie's key ring and headed for the stairs.

Chapter Twenty

The main room downstairs was still. Piped-in ambient music played very softly in the background. Drake was still at his post, and I caught him yawning. He smiled sheepishly when our eyes met.

Two players, Derek Bartolo and Gunnar Larsen, sat at the bar nursing drinks and talking in subdued voices.

At a table set up in the area off the lobby, Rich Haskins and Kenneth Chen leaned over a chess board. They were moving and snatching pieces off the board with amazing speed.

The dining table had been cleared and an older man was wiping it down. This must be Francisco. He looked up as I approached and straightened up. His eyes were red, and he looked like he'd just lost his best friend.

"You are Gracie, right? Can I get you anything?"

"No, Francisco." I waved him over toward the kitchen and lowered my voice. "I wanted to ask you some questions about last night. I'm trying to do what I can to help Reggie."

The man swallowed and a look of strong emotion passed over his face.

"Then, please, ask me."

"What time was your shift last night? Did you prepare food or serve?"

"I worked my usual time. 2:00 p.m. to 10:00 p.m. I brought out the courses and did clean up like I always do."

"You served each course to everyone at the table. You would notice if somebody wasn't in their seat."

"Yes. And last night, all seats were filled when I brought out the salad. With the main dish, there were a few people missing. Two, I think."

Salad would be around 6:50 p.m., if I remembered correctly. He probably wouldn't remember who was missing, but he would have brought out the osso bucco at around 7:15 p.m. Mehta was still there when we were served the main course, and I remembered him picking at it. I tried to think of who in the group wasn't there at that time.

"Do you remember where the empty seats were?" I asked. "Can you show me?"

Francisco walked around the table slowly, trying to visualize last night's setup.

"A man with black glasses. Older. He was sitting here," he said as he walked toward a seat at the end of the table nearest the stairs. Then Francisco suddenly looked over at the bar.

"That man," he whispered to me.

This was not a surprise. Derek Bartolo had been gone most of the evening. And he wasn't exactly a fan of Mehta.

"Then there was another man with glasses. Young but with light, short hair. Very skinny."

Trey Godwin. I hadn't noticed him missing at all. For

all I knew he could have gone to the restroom. Or even to the bar. I'd ask Drake.

Mehta had excused himself to go upstairs around seven thirty.

There were a few pieces that needed to be in place in order to figure this out.

I needed to know, though, if anyone had gone upstairs before or shortly after Mehta. Had somebody been waiting for him?

Younghee had been on the stairs, saying she was worried about Mehta, maybe fifteen minutes after he'd gone to his room. She could have gone up to his room with him. And maybe she did.

But if she'd killed him, there was no way she could get out of the room with the lock and chain still set.

I was covering the same territory the chief and Brad did in their investigation.

And not making any more progress than they did.

After thanking Francisco for his help, I went over to Drake. He looked tired and sad, and like he just wanted to go home.

Derek and Gunnar had finished up at the bar and were headed toward the back stairs, the route that led to Reggie's office and to the floors of rooms.

The back stairs had helped me and my friend Elana last October, when I was trying to dodge the two Russian spies.

On their way toward the stairs, Gunnar made a joke that he drank so much beer his bladder wasn't going to hold it on the trip up the stairs. He went into the men's restroom at the bottom of the stairs. Derek took out his phone and started scrolling as he waited for him.

You should remember this, something inside me said.

Okay, fine, subconscious.

I rolled my eyes at my subconscious.

"Hey, Drake." I walked up and leaned on the bar. "Weird question. I wanted to ask you something. Did you see that tall, thin player with blond hair go past here toward the back stairs last night? It would have been during the dinner."

He paused to think. "I know who you mean. He wears glasses."

I nodded.

"I don't think I saw him. It was busy, and I could have missed him." He frowned. "Sorry, Gracie."

I thanked him and decided to go up the back stairs to see if I could track Kimo down on his rounds. I was getting sleepy. I thought if I could check out my room without collapsing on the bed, I'd do it.

The back stairs took me to Reggie's office and my room next to it. I pulled out the keys and found the one marked #2-0.

I turned the key in the rattly old lock and opened the door to a small room with a tiny bathroom-like window. One side of the small room was piled with guitar cases, meaning there wasn't much room to move around at all.

But the twin bed looked comfortable enough and made me reflexively yawn. I'd been awake since 4:30 a.m.

While I was in the room, I stretched out on the bed and checked my phone. I missed cuddling with my little dog.

Willow had sent me the room assignments for last night. I scrolled through them. Floor 3 was mostly couples—Derek and Kendra Bartolo; Gunnar Larsen and his wife, Emma; Kenneth and Carrie Chen; and the Haskins.

Floor 2 was Mehta in room 8 and everyone else. Patrick Bowman and Trey Godwin were in rooms 7 and 9, on either side of Mehta's room. Maya Singh and her mother were in room 5, and Younghee in room 6.

I left my room and went in search of Kimo. I found him when I got to the bathroom at the end of the hall. He was scrubbing a sink while listening to music on his ear buds. It took me a few seconds to get his attention.

"Oh, hey. You must be Gracie," he said after he took the buds out and stood up. He was wearing a large, red Bruno Mars t-shirt. "Willow said you wanted to ask me some questions about last night."

"Do you have time?" I asked. "Would you be up for a quick talk downstairs by the bar?"

His eyes crinkled up. "Nobody's here to see if I'm doing my job or not. Sure."

We walked down the front stairs.

We sat down in front of the fireplace. Drake brought us a couple of glasses of ice water.

"You were working last night."

"Yeah. I'm housekeeper, janitor, and sometimes repairman on the night shift. Been coming here after my day job for five years. I bring up sheets, pillows, blankets, or space heaters in the winter, when guests need them. I get the A/C going when guests are too hot. I clean the public restrooms and sometimes the rooms if they're not occupied."

"You know these rooms well then," I said, picturing Mehta's room as I remembered it. "Can you think of any place in room 8 where someone could hide if they wanted to?"

"Well, only the bathroom." Kimo leaned back in his chair, which creaked loudly. "I can't think of anywhere else."

"There's a closet near the front door in that room. With a narrow door. You know what I'm talking about?"

Kimo laughed heartily. "That's not a closet. It has a furnace in it. It comes from the original old house. Ain't no person gonna fit in there."

I wanted to see it myself now. But that would require me going back into the room. Which was a crime scene.

"Thanks, Kimo. Do you remember seeing anyone up on the second floor when dinner was being served? Like between 7:15 and 8:00 p.m.?"

He nodded. "Sure. There was this beautiful girl. I think she's one of the players. Asian. I saw her washing her hands in the second-floor bathroom, then she went downstairs."

"See anybody else?"

"Oh, and there was a skinny white dude with glasses. His hair was almost white, too. He saw me and then hurried down the hall to get to the back stairs. But he'd been standing right by the *front* stairs. Real weird, huh?"

Chapter Twenty-One

I stood in the hallway, ticking off boxes in my mind like I was playing the game of *Clue*.

Based on what I had found out, I could make some deductions. I played with the facts and where they fit —to see if I could piece together a full picture of the events of last night.

I had to see the room again. I dreaded it.

I went to the door of room 8, where the chief and Brad had strung up yellow DO NOT CROSS tape across the door frame.

I pushed the tape out of the way, then turned the key in the lock and opened the door.

The room was stuffy and had a weird metallic smell that made me gag. Out of the corner of my eye, I saw the bed but avoided looking at it. I covered my hand with tissues from a box on the indigo dresser to avoid leaving fingerprints, then I turned the knob to open the bathroom door.

Aside from Mehta's toiletries and toothbrush on the counter, there was nothing much to see. I flicked on the lights to see if there was any evidence someone had left behind. I looked in the deep iron bathtub and saw a shower mat had been laid out in it, so it looked like Mehta or someone had used the shower.

Could someone have gone into Mehta's room with him, maybe to have a conversation, and then killed him? They could have hidden in the bathtub afterwards. While we were rushing to Mehta and trying to see if he was alive, the person could have quietly slipped out the door.

Only one problem. It was hard to imagine anybody getting out of that very deep, antique tub quickly and quietly.

If I remembered clearly, the bathroom door had been open while Reggie and I were in the room. It was unlikely someone could have been hiding there.

Then I looked at the narrow furnace door, which still had a shirt hanging on the doorknob.

It stood out to me because it was the narrowest door I'd ever seen.

I kept the toilet paper wrapped on my hand and pulled open the furnace closet door.

The old furnace was cold, not in use in August's heat, if ever. It took up almost all that space. I turned on the light on my phone and flashed it around.

There could be just room enough for the right person.

As I pulled my phone back to turn it off, the light flashed on something red on the floor of the space.

I reached down with a tissue to grab a red pencil, the kind the players had been using at the tournament to document their moves.

I looked for something to put it in, so it could be checked for fingerprints. I couldn't find anything that made a good evidence envelope. I went into the bathroom and found a plastic bag used for taking up ice from the bar to the room. I slipped the pencil into the bag and knotted the end firmly.

I was exhausted and trying to keep my eyes open. My body wanted to sleep, but my brain was pursuing the solution to this murder, and I didn't want to quit.

I snapped some pictures on my phone of the furnace space and the pencil in the bag. Then I tucked the bag into my purse. I sent the photos to my email and copied the chief and Brad.

I saw I had a text from Mayor C.

Reggie's in the city hall cell tonight

It wasn't the best of accommodations, but hey, it wasn't the county jail.

After several minutes in Mehta's room, my lungs craved fresh air. I opened the door to leave and went out into the hall.

I leaned against the wall and took in deep gulps of fresh air. Then I continued down the hall in the direction of my little room.

The Riverside seemed to be sleeping. All was quiet. Drake must have closed the bar and gone home.

Kimo must have signed off his shift.

I felt suddenly very alone. But the creaks of the old building made me fear that maybe I *wasn't* alone.

I saw my door and went to unlock it. Key in my hand, I was suddenly confronted with something I couldn't comprehend. I was so tired, it took me a while to figure out what my eyes were seeing.

Someone was standing in front of the door.

Thin and pale as a ghost against the white door. A ghost with glasses.

He was holding a knife. It looked a lot like the high-end knives the kitchen staff used. Like the knives used to cut Beck's cakes.

"Gracie," the voice said. "How funny. I didn't know you were a guest here. Why don't we go inside?"

Chapter Twenty-Two

Since Trey was holding a knife and all, I wasn't going to say, "I'm beat…so I'll have to say *no*."

We walked into my small room.

With his knife pointing the way, Trey directed me to sit on the bed. He took a seat on an antique wooden chair across from me.

"What were you doing in Mehta's room?"

"I know now. Reggie didn't kill Mehta," I said simply. "You did."

"What are you even talking about?" he asked with a very staged air of being offended. "I had no access to the room. Reggie did. He is the only one besides Mehta who had a key. The killer's been arrested, and justice has been served."

I was already feeling angry and sad because Reggie had gone completely willingly. He'd even tried to make the arrest as easy as possible for the chief.

"You went up the back stairs, didn't you? Said you were going to the restroom, but then you went to Mehta's room, and he let you in," I blurted out. I was so tired, I barely knew where these words were coming from. "You killed him and hid in the furnace closet. You were there all along, when Reggie and I got into the room, weren't you? Then when we were trying to figure out if Mehta was alive, you made your escape through the open door."

"The locked room, greatest of all mysteries." Trey smiled, looking very proud of himself. "You know, I play in these tournaments, against geniuses. People who think they're so much smarter than me. No matter how hard I work, they check me. Do you know how hard I've tried to beat these people? I've studied for years. I've tried to memorize all the plays, all the gambits. I deserved a victory at this tournament. And who was the first one to beat me? Andrew Mehta." His voice rose to a crescendo and it was loud. I hoped it was loud enough to wake up guests in the rooms on this floor.

Then I remembered—my room was next to Reggie's office, much farther away from the row of regular rooms on the floor. Nobody would hear him at all.

Trey continued on, talking about his losses, describing them in detail. He cited names and places, even coordinates of squares on the chess board for the moves. He mumbled to himself. "I'm smarter than all of them. After all, I took out the competition last night. Nobody else did that."

I thought of the quote Younghee told me about: *Poets don't go mad. Chess players do.*

"Trey, why did you try to frame Reggie? I know you put his champagne glass from dinner on the nightstand."

"Of course I did. He didn't even know it was missing." He snorted, then continued.

"On Friday I heard Mehta outside The Riverside, talking on his phone to someone. He said he was going to confront Reggie. Turns out Reggie did something really bad years ago. Stole a ton of money. Then he changed his identity. He was the perfect one to pin Mehta's death on." Trey lifted his hands in a helpless gesture. "I'd be stupid to pass that up. And I'm definitely *not* stupid."

His voice grew louder and more insistent, as if he were trying hard to convince himself not me. "I planned the perfect crime. When I saw Mehta go upstairs during dinner, I went up the back stairs. I knocked on his door and said I wanted to thank him for teaching me so much—in that game where he beat me. Mehta had just taken some pills and he didn't resist. I told him he should lie down. He did, and that's when I pulled out the knife. Then when I heard people coming upstairs, I looked around and found the furnace closet. When you and Reggie came in and went to Mehta's body, I just walked out the open door. "

I shook my head, and my face must have showed my disgust for Trey. "You don't know Reggie. You have no idea what Reggie's situation was. And now an innocent man, a good man, is in jail for murder because of you."

"Don't you lecture me, Gracie. Don't act like you're smarter than me. Everyone thinks they're smarter than me! It's not true." Trey's voice rose and his face turned from white to pastel pink. He looked like an angry bunny. He held the knife like a dagger, and it glinted under the overhead light.

First, I heard the footsteps on the back stairs, coming closer. Then pounding on the door.

"Open up, this is River Grove Police. We're armed. Come out now or we'll enter by force."

No shots were fired. The chief opened the door slowly but easily, since it hadn't been locked. He came in followed by Brad Castro. Standing behind both of them was Kimo.

"You okay, Gracie?" the chief asked. I nodded.

Trey dropped the knife and leaned against the wall, his hands raised. The chief quickly handcuffed him. I told the chief and Brad about Trey hiding in the closet while Reggie and I attended to Mehta. "Thanks for the photos, Gracie," Brad acknowledged. "We'll be checking the pencil for fingerprints."

"Trey Godwin, you are under arrest for making terroristic threats and for false imprisonment. You are also under suspicion for the murder of Andrew Mehta." The chief launched into reading the pale young man his rights.

Then the chief and Brad Castro marched Trey down the back stairs. I heard Trey's threats float up as the three of them descended, like a reprise of Reggie's words last night.

"Get your hands off me. I'll sue you—I'll sue you all. I'm smarter than all of you!"

Kimo stood in the doorway, a look of relief on his face. "Yeah. So my last job of the night is cleaning Reggie's office. I heard that guy talking so loud in here. I heard what he said about Reggie, and I got worried for you. I figured I should call 911."

❦

Nobody at The Riverside slept much that night.

I texted Nate and told him what happened. He called immediately and told me he and my dad would head over after dropping Biga off at Mary Jo's.

The arrival of the chief and Brad and all the footsteps up and down the stairs woke up the second-floor guests. They came out of their rooms. The buzz of loud conversation in the hallway must have carried to the third floor. Soon the guests from upstairs all came down. We ended up convening in Reggie's purple conference room next door.

Nate and my dad eased into the room and took seats near the window after I started telling my story.

I briefly told everyone what had happened—that Trey had been arrested and had tried to frame Reggie.

"I don't get it. Why would Trey do this?" Aiden McAlister asked, as he leaned back in the papasan chair.

"He said people had been putting him down for years, saying he copied other players' moves and wasn't a very good chess player. Sounds like he finally flipped out and lashed out—at the person everyone thought of as the smartest player in the tournament."

Derek Bartolo snorted and rolled his eyes. "And who said Mehta was the smart player? He used other players' moves, too."

"And he used AI to prepare for his games," Patrick Bowman said, crossing his arms against his chest defensively.

Younghee was curled up in a chair near the doorway in her nightgown and pink slippers. Her eyes were puffy from crying.

"Drew was a brilliant player," she said quietly. "You were all so busy hating on him, coming up with ways to cut him down to size, because you were jealous."

The room went quiet for a while.

Later, I sat down with Younghee and told her what Mehta had said to the group of male players surrounding him by Beck's cake: *Younghee's the player I'm most afraid of.*

She pressed her lips together and her eyes watered up. "I would never have guessed that."

She went on to confide more about her relationship and how she was dealing with her loss. She needed to talk, even if it was for the comfort of having someone listen, a witness to what she'd been through, this weekend and for the past year with Mehta.

There are men who can do these conversations—Nate's good at it. But sometimes a woman speaks in a language that's more easily understood by another woman.

"Good luck tomorrow morning, Younghee." I hugged her.

"Thank you, Gracie. Thank you for everything." She yawned and padded up the stairs to her room in her slippers.

Gradually, everyone went back to their rooms, though there were a few conversations amongst the players, reconstructing games they'd played over the weekend. My dad joined in with them excitedly, as if we hadn't just witnessed the dramatic arrest of a murderer.

Since revisiting moves in a game is my least favorite thing to do, Nate and I went next door to my room. I shut the door.

He looked down at the twin bed as if trying to figure out how he'd fit on it.

"I don't think this is a one size fits all. I can sleep on the couch out in the conference room," he said with a faint smile. "Your dad said he's going to make a bed of pillows in the papasan chair in there."

"Stay," I commanded. My "nice" filter had disappeared with my tiredness. "I want to be with you."

We gingerly laid down on our sides in the small bed and just managed to fit. We laughed at our precarious positioning on the bed. Nate's long legs nearly touched the bank of guitars at the end of the bed.

I lay my head down near his chest. I felt his breath go in and out, like the sound of waves on the beach rolling in and rolling out.

And that led to my dream that night, after a very crazy two days.

I was on the beach at Santa Cruz, in the warm sun. Nate was next to me, intent on building a sandcastle just for birds. The waves rolled in and receded in a soothing rhythm that made me sleepy and at peace.

Then in the distance, I saw someone walking toward us. He got closer and closer until I recognized the face, the hair, and even the eyes.

He wasn't wearing sunglasses. He was grinning, like this was the best day ever.

"Good morning, Gracie. I'm back."

Chapter Twenty-Three

DAY 4
River Grove Chess Tournament
Labor Day – Monday, September 1

Pairings
****REVISED****

Patrick Bowman – Derek Bartolo
Maya Singh – Rich Haskins
Kenneth Chen – Aiden McAlister
Younghee Park – Gunnar Larsen

The next morning, I woke up in the small bed, disoriented.

Early morning light filtered in from the small window. I got up and looked out at the alley, to the green-space beyond. The sun peeked through the light layer of fog as it threaded its way through the redwoods.

I looked at my phone. 6:00 a.m.

Nate was now on the floor, snoring on a comforter he must have found in the closet.

I missed Biga.

He was probably busy licking Mary Jo's kitchen floor right now. She would bring Biga back after the community tournament.

I'd fallen asleep in my clothes, which really needed to be changed. Maybe I could rummage through the lost and found in Reggie's office.

There was only one thing on my mind right now. *Coffee.*

I went into the bathroom and splashed my face, then patted it dry with a towel. I put on my shoes and headed down the back stairs, trying to be quiet.

None of the players seemed to be up yet—no surprise.

The staff was rattling pans and stacking plates in the kitchen. I didn't see a coffee Cambro set up in the dining area, so I popped my head into the kitchen and smiled at the crew of three getting ready for the day.

"Hey, have you made the coffee yet?"

"Gracie!" There were smiles on the faces of Reggie's kitchen staff.

"We heard what happened last night," said a man with a nametag reading *Jose*. "We're so glad you're okay."

Chef Jorge, looking tired but happy, went to the espresso machine. "I will make you a latte, Gracie. You sit. We'll bring you breakfast."

"Thank you for making sure the right guy got arrested." A young woman with a tag reading *Ariana* was sniffling and smiling at the same time.

The kitchen staff basically pushed me out of the kitchen while thanking me. Thanks for what? I defended my life last night. The confrontation with Trey Godwin could have easily gone the wrong way. I was just happy Reggie would be set free today.

In a few minutes, Chef Jorge came out with a tray loaded with goodies. There was a beautiful looking latte with a heart poured into the foam, a plate with *two* kouign-amanns, and a bowl of fresh strawberries.

"Thank you so much, Chef. This looks wonderful."

Jorge's lower lip was trembling. "Reggie called to say they are letting him go. The chief will bring him soon."

I started crying, too.

Chef Jorge went back into the kitchen.

I sat back and let out a deep sigh of thanks.

Then I started in on my coffee.

I had just finished kouign-amann #1 when the front doors of The Riverside opened. Reggie, sans sunglasses, walked in with the chief beside him.

I got up and ran up the steps to meet them. I hugged Reggie. My tears left a wet spot on his black shirt.

"Welcome back. It's so good to see you, Reggie."

He smelled like dust and office supplies.

"Gracie, thank you for figuring out what happened. I still can't believe he was in the furnace closet when we were in the room."

When I let go of Reggie, the chief pulled me to the side.

"I've got to take care of a few things. By the way, I took Trey Godwin down to the county jail in Santa Cruz." He grimaced. "They can have him."

AFTER A SHOWER and change of clothes, Reggie came back downstairs and took a seat at my table. With a smile and a half hug, Jorge brought him coffee and a blueberry muffin on a plate.

When Jorge went back into the kitchen, Reggie looked around and said to me in a low voice. "So you know."

"The chief told me everything." I paused, then felt like I needed to confess. "I'm sorry, Reggie. I was in your office last night, and I saw the letter from your mother."

Reggie's mouth twisted as if he was in pain. Then it resolved into a mischievous grin. "I should have known you'd find it. You are, as the chief says, a snoop." His voice turned quiet. "A friend passed her letter on to me. After my dad passed away, I went back East to spend some time with my mother."

Something in me loosened when I heard that. "I'm so glad you did, Reggie."

"In fact, my old friend is coming today," he continued, tapping his phone to check a message. "I thought he was trying to expose me, but now I know that wasn't true. He wanted to help me."

"Reggie, I don't know everything. But I am glad you're not a bank CEO. I can't think of anything further from who you are."

"You and me both." He chuckled, but his eyes looked distant, preoccupied. "I don't know what I'm going to tell people, Gracie."

"You don't have to tell them anything. Only if you feel ready."

"I'll think about it," Reggie said. "Meanwhile, my friend will be here for the last part of the tournament. I haven't seen him in almost sixty years. I don't know what I'll say. Or worse, what he'll say."

"But it's good that he's coming?"

Reggie looked at the table and then up at me. I was still

getting used to him without the sunglasses. It was a different look, older and softer.

"I'm nervous, but I think it's good. Sarkis is my friend."

Reggie had to catch up with his staff after being gone, so he left for the kitchen. When Willow Barrett came in, Reggie came back to the dining area and the two sat down at the long table to go over details for the day and how checkout would be handled.

And I went upstairs to see if sleeping beauty was awake.

I found him sitting cross-legged on the floor, playing one of The Riverside's guitars.

Chapter Twenty-Four

As players made their way down the stairs to the breakfast table, the last day of the tournament officially started.

On Labor Day morning, with some help from Kimo, who was here again bright and early, the divided sides of the saloon's main hall came down, and the lunch line was dismantled.

The kitchen staff set up the long dining table as a communal breakfast space. Bowls of fresh fruit; plates of pastries, bacon, and sausage; mini breakfast burritos from the kitchen; and a platter of sliced Laughing Loaf breads—including brioche and my walnut, whole-wheat biga loaf, which Reggie had requested.

The chief and Brad came by at 8:00 a.m. for another interview with me about the events of the past two nights.

I hadn't had a chance to go home, but Nate and my father had made a run to our houses to get fresh clothes for us. After a shower, I came downstairs feeling like a new person.

And excited about this last day of the tournament.

This morning it was as if a player had tapped the timer clock for the tournament and all had been reset. Andrew Mehta's absence was felt, but the players had one last chance to immerse themselves in the game they loved.

Focusing on your next move on the board, it's hard to mull over the losses; you're worried about what's right in front of you—keeping your king protected.

The players who gathered around the table for breakfast seemed giddy and relieved. Kendra Bartolo rested her hand on Derek's shoulder and the two were showing signs of affection for each other. Derek seemed talkative and in good spirits again.

Maya Singh and her mother sat at the end of the table, keeping to themselves. I was surprised they'd stayed. I'm sure Maya's mother regretted bringing her young daughter to the event.

The "boys" (that is Aiden, Kenneth, and Patrick) plundered the breakfast burritos as they traded game strategies across the table. Rich Haskins and his wife had a trail map for Henry Cowell State Park spread out on the table and were talking about going for a hike in the redwoods after the tournament finished up.

Nate came down the stairs, his hair damp and beginning to form waves. He pulled the chair out next to me and kissed my cheek. He hadn't shaved, so his face was scratchy. He smelled like The Riverside's patchouli soap.

"Good morning, love," he murmured in my ear, making me feel tingly.

Finally, Reggie came down the back stairs, stopping off at the bar to confer with Drake.

When guests at the table saw him, all conversation stopped. They watched as he approached the group. He stood at the head of the table, my dad to his right.

"Welcome back, Reggie!" Derek Bartolo called out. Reggie was back in his all-black uniform again, despite predictions of more 90-degree temperatures.

"Welcome to the last day of the first ever River Grove Chess Tournament." Reggie smiled wryly. "Can I tell you how happy I am to be here?"

Everyone gathered at the table clapped. The boys contingent let out a series of wolfish howls.

"We're glad you're here, too, Reggie," Aiden McAlister shouted.

"Here's the program for today," Reggie said, looking around the table. "Our final round will start at 10 a.m. The pairings have been texted to you all."

"Obviously, we had to make changes to the pairings. This hasn't been easy for you all. But I'm glad you've all stayed, despite what's happened. Thank you also, to my partner in this, John, for stepping in last night and doing double duty in my absence."

Players around the table checked their phones to see their pairings for their final match. Some cheered. Some looked around the table to find their opponent, then smiled at each other in recognition.

Younghee, sitting next to me, put down her phone and turned to me. "I'm playing Gunnar Larsen," she said in a low voice. "I'm happy with that."

After Reggie's arrival, the air in the room changed. The tenseness was gone, the fear that had gripped everyone had dissipated. There was a ripple of excitement in the room.

Since they'd been awake till 2:00 a.m., everyone at the table looked exhausted, their eyes droopy and clothes rumpled. But in a scrappy, determined way, they looked forward to playing each other.

As we finished up breakfast, I watched as an audiovisual technician readjusted the display screens, so a full group of spectators could watch the final matches.

Once this final round was done, the room would be rearranged, and tables set up for the informal community tournament.

As 10:00 a.m. approached, players made their way to the four tables set up in the middle of the saloon, their scorebooks and red mechanical pencils in hand. The boards were ready, and the digital timers were set up on the correct side of the board—to the right of each player playing black pieces.

Then at 9:55 a.m., the front doors of The Riverside flew open. A short, stocky man in a grey suit set down his suitcase with a thud.

Reggie swayed suddenly and gripped the pillar he was standing next to. His face tightened. I knew this was probably a good thing for Reggie, but it would not be easy.

Sarkis Kaprelian had arrived.

Chapter Twenty-Five

Reggie stood, steadying himself. His brown eyes full of fear, he took a deep breath and, a little stiffly, walked toward the man.

Most people in the room seemed to sense something unusual was happening. Yet another thing, in addition to the disturbing and crazy events that had happened in this small, out-of-the way town.

Reggie reached the man. I couldn't hear their conversation. I tried to focus on Reggie and this older man as I imagined the words exchanged between them. Sarkis's hands moved, gesturing emphatically as he talked. Reggie nodded and occasionally smiled.

Suddenly they hugged with a fierceness that I'd only seen between men in other cultures—Mediterranean or Hispanic. They held each other, and Reggie put his head down on the man's shoulder. His shoulders convulsed. He was sobbing.

The players, seated at their tables, looked around at each other uneasily as if wondering: "Should we play?" My dad got up from his spot in the skittles area and went to each table to talk to the players. He spoke to them in a low voice. Each player sat back in their seat and waited quietly. Maya Singh's eyes looked terrified as she sat across from Rich Haskins, ready for her match. Her first big tournament —First a murder. Now what was *this*?

I glanced at my phone. It was now 10:15 a.m. Nate reached down and held my hand—I think because he was a little nervous. I looked up at him, not knowing what to say.

After a few more minutes, Reggie and Sarkis walked to the stage set up near the bar. Reggie picked up a micro- phone and switched it on.

"Thank you for your patience. Allow me to introduce a very old friend of mine. This is Sarkis Kaprelian, one of my oldest friends. And Andrew Mehta's chess coach."

Gasps arose and conversation rumbled through the room.

Reggie continued. "For a number of reasons, Sarkis and I have not spoken in almost sixty years. That is entirely my fault, not his. We grew up playing chess and went to regional and national competitions together."

Sarkis grabbed the microphone away from his old friend.

"There is something my friend is not telling you. He was the US champion in 1969 and was heading to the World Championships in Moscow." The room erupted in lively chatter now.

Sarkis continued. "Then he quit chess."

Silence. The boys contingent could be heard murmur- ing, *what the hell?*

Reggie took the mic back.

"I gave it up. I felt pressure in another area of my life. So I gave up everything. I didn't want to let anyone else down. I ran away from people who cared about me." Reggie put his hand on Sarkis's shoulder. "Just remember when you play today. Chess is fun, exciting, and challenging. But it's a game. I want to thank John over here, for reminding me of that. And helping me to love it again."

He looked at my dad, who nodded and kept his feelings neatly under wraps as usual. Sarkis took out a handkerchief and noisily proceeded to let the tears flow.

"Without further delay," Reggie said with a smile. "Let's finish this tournament. Players, go ahead and start your games."

Nate and I found seats in the skittles area, and I leaned against Nate while I cried quietly to myself. It was happy crying, something I'd experienced a lot of in the past two years. We watched the play on the screens, but I was thinking less of the games we were watching and more about what had happened this weekend. And about Reggie's making peace with his past.

Nate, however, was very engaged in what was happening on the screen.

"Younghee's going to do it. Look at that move. Checkmate. She's just beaten Gunnar, and he's a good player. She's got the points to win now."

In a few minutes, Reggie and my dad announced Younghee Park as the winner of the first River Grove Chess Championship. Applause erupted throughout the room. Tears ran down Younghee's cheeks, but I could also see her smiling through them.

Maya Singh shyly approached Younghee at the lunch feast that followed. Younghee invited her to sit down, and they started talking and continued for almost an hour.

I thought about all Younghee had been through and how lonely chess tournaments must have been for her growing up. I remembered somebody saying to me once:

Happy are those who give what they have not been given.

As she talked excitedly to Maya about her game, about tournaments in general—and even about dating, Younghee finally looked happy.

AFTER LUNCH—WHICH I was happy to have *no* responsibility for—Reggie's staff cleared off the dining table and set out coffee Cambros, beverages, and desserts. They filled the large open floor of The Riverside with chairs and tables for the community tournament.

I took a seat in the spectator area, excited to see Nate and my dad play. I was also curious about who from River Grove and the surrounding areas would come to play.

A little before 1 p.m., a steady stream of people flooded in through the saloon's double doors, many of whom I recognized but some I didn't. The chief had come in with Mayor C, followed by Hank and Victor from the Key Haus. Then Beck's older brother Korben came in, along with Kirk Schiffer, my best friend Elana's husband.

My dad had told me he and Reggie sent invites to local chess organizations, including clubs at local high schools. There were quite a few teenagers. I recognized some of the older teens: Chloe came in with Jeb Walker. Not far behind, Sky Robbins, wearing a pink Hello Kitty baseball cap, entered with Dakota Li. When it turned out Jeb and Sky were paired for the first match, Jeb groaned so loudly I could hear it from the spectators' area. "Who set *this* up?"

The two young men had grown up as childhood friends, but their very different personalities had caused many clashes between them in high school. Now, surprisingly, they sat down across from each other and calmly started their game.

Nate came over to me, a cup of coffee in each hand. He planted a kiss on my cheek. "I'm heading over to play Maya Singh. You looked like you needed more caffeine." He handed me a cup. I wrapped my hands around it gratefully.

"I do. And good luck. Maya's really good."

Among the community players, there was a face that I didn't recognize, a man who looked like he was approaching forty. He had scruffy light brown hair and wore big, large-framed glasses and a t-shirt with a Rubik's Cube on it. When I saw him, I pulled my dad aside.

"Who's the guy with the Rubik's t-shirt? He looks familiar, but I can't place him."

My dad grinned. "You don't recognize him? Gracie, I'm surprised. I figured out who he was before you did."

We must be living in an alternate universe if my dad was beating me in the area of facial recognition.

"He's here to help us." My dad cleared his throat and lowered his voice. "With our *Patrick problem*."

I focused in on the table where Patrick Bowman had taken his seat across from Rubik's Cube Man. The two began setting up their pieces to start the game.

It must have been my lack of sleep last night. Gradually, I saw the features, the hair, and the scruffy neck beard and figured it out.

"That's Jeremy Lavalle," I whispered excitedly to my dad. "He's trying to blend in with his environment. He's convincing as a chess nerd."

"He called this morning to tell me he had an idea. He's posing as one of my former teaching assistants."

Now I was really curious. I wished I could listen in on their conversation.

My dad was assigned to the next two matches. First, he'd play Patrick Bowman, then Sarkis Kaprelian. I went over to the seating area, where Chloe Westerman was talking to Dakota Li.

"Gracie," Chloe reached over to give me a side hug. "I just saw you yesterday, but it feels like a century since then. Are you okay after everything that happened? My grandpa told me about last night."

I sighed, but it turned into a long yawn. "It was scary, but I'm fine now. A little low on sleep. But who needs sleep when there's coffee, right?"

There was a big difference between the champions tournament and the informal community tournament. In this competition, players laughed and chatted with each other. Whenever somebody won, Reggie picked up the microphone and announced the winner, and everyone in the room cheered.

After the first matches ended, my dad went to play Patrick, and Nate sat down across from Maya. After a round of cheers for Jeb's victory, Sky came our way and wearily plopped down behind us, his arm resting on the back of Dakota's chair. He'd flipped the Hello Kitty hat around backwards, so he looked like a rap star.

"I'm giving up on chess," he moaned. "That was painful."

"Jeb is very competitive," Chloe said, a note of pride in her voice.

"What are you up to, after your roller coaster job at the Boardwalk?" I asked Sky. "Will you work and go to school?"

He sat up. "I've got a job here in town, working as a caregiver three afternoons a week. My therapist told me about it."

"Who are you a caregiver for?" I asked, very curious.

"Cookoff champion Scotty Baxter. I kinda like the old guy, so I said yes."

"Perfect! You two will get along well."

Honestly? I couldn't have arranged a better match.

"He insists my name is Steve," Sky said with a shrug. "But he also thinks I'm funny. I like hanging out with people who laugh at my jokes. If they pay me, even better."

I tried to keep a straight face. "Just remember, *Steve*, when you're with Scotty, you have to be the responsible one."

After his game with Patrick ended, my dad came over and sat down next to me.

"Well, that was interesting, Gracie." My father raised his eyebrows and gave me a strange smile. "Patrick told me he was happy that I reunited with my biological mother after my retirement. He thought it was touching that I chose to take on the original name she gave me at birth."

"*That* was Jeremy's story?" I stifled a laugh. Patrick was now setting up pieces for his game with Jeb.

My dad chuckled. "My biological mother would have had a good laugh at that."

"That explanation seemed to satisfy him?"

"Very much so." My dad looked relieved.

He nodded at Sarkis, who'd sat down at an empty table and was lining up his pieces.

"I've got to go. I'm playing Mehta's chess tutor," he said with a smile. "I'm definitely heading for a loss."

After he finished his games, Nate and I got drinks from Drake at the bar and made our way upstairs to Reggie's balcony. There was so much to say, so much information to share. We were too overwhelmed and tired to talk about any of it.

Silence felt good.

In the cool shade, we lay back in Reggie's Adirondack chairs. We took our shoes off and stretched out our feet, as we listened to the San Luciano River tumbling over the rocks below.

As the afternoon wore on, a light breeze rustled through the trees, while children giggled and splashed in delight, and parents admonished them from their camp chairs on the riverbank.

When we finished our drinks, we promptly fell asleep.

Thank you

Thank you for reading Naan the Wiser!

If you enjoyed this book, please consider leaving a review or rating on Amazon, Goodreads, or the book review site of your choice.

I truly value the time you take to do this, and it makes my author heart very happy.

Find a typo or inaccuracy?

If you come across any typos or inaccuracies in this book or any of my others, I'd appreciate it if you could let me know using this contact form:

https://victoriakazarian.com/contact

Thanks!

Also by Victoria Kazarian

Drop Dead Bread - Laughing Loaf Mystery #1

Bread to Rights - Laughing Loaf Mystery #2

Trouble You Don't Knead - Laughing Loaf Mystery #3

Sourdough & Cyanide - Laughing Loaf Mystery #4

Proof of Death - Laughing Loaf Mystery #5

An Oven Beyond - Laughing Loaf Mystery #6

Shot Through the Tart - Laughing Loaf Mystery #7

Stop, Drop and Rolls: A Laughing Loaf Bakery Short Mystery (prequel novella)

Stay tuned for Laughing Loaf #9 - Rye or Die, coming soon!

TRADITIONAL MYSTERY

writing as VL Kazarian

(Detectives Ruiz, Grasso and Flores):

Swift Horses Racing – Silicon Valley Murder Book 1

Across the Red Sky – Silicon Valley Murder Book 2

A Tree of Poison – Silicon Valley Murder Book 3

About Victoria Kazarian

Victoria Kazarian lives and writes in San Jose, California. After working for years as a Silicon Valley marketing professional, she taught high school English and actually owned a bread bakery of her own called The Laughing Loaf. When she's not writing, she enjoys baking artisan breads and forcing her children and dog to go on road trips to the Pacific Northwest.

See what she's up to at victoriakazarian.com

You can contact Victoria—or perhaps leave a message for Gracie Markley herself—at TheLaughingLoaf@ gmail.com

Acknowledgments

Thank you, friends, for enjoying and supporting this series, and the quirky town and people of River Grove.

The cool thing about creating a fictional place is that people begin to look fondly upon something that is a complete figment of my imagination. You honor me with your willingness to care about these characters and spend time with them.

I could not have written this book without a lot of support.

My editor/idea generator, Honest Magpie, has been a great help—thank you. As well as my husband, Pete, who is always up for eating Indian food with me and playing games. The antics of our pesky chihuahua mix, Peewee, give me inspiration for the kind of trouble Biga would get into.

Thank you to my beta readers—Faye Friesen Myers, Kerry Nozicka, Amanda Giles, and Karen Bowers. And to Chris Anderson, my timekeeper and lifesaver, who catches my inevitable timeline issues and even has ideas for fixing them.

And to my proofreaders, Mary Ann Askins, Karen Stevenson, and Vivian Gudan. Your eyes see what I gloss over. Thank you for using your special gift to find these things.

And thank you to Sisters in Crime, both my local chapter, SinC Coastal Cruisers, and SinC National. The write-ins have kept me accountable with my writing time and the coming-alongside-each-other that we do is so encouraging. I love that we can support each other in what often feels like a solitary profession.

Are you in a book club?

Interested in reading any of The Laughing Loaf Bakery Mysteries with your book club? I'd love to appear at your book club online - and possibly in person, if you're in the San Francisco Bay Area.

Contact me at thelaughingloaf@gmail.com

Laughing Loaf Bakery Recipes

Naan (and how to make a naanini)

Chess Square Cookies (Shackrutor)

Homemade Chai Tea Mix

Naan (and how to make a naanini)

Time: Approximately 1 hour, 45 minutes
Makes 10 naan

Ingredients
1/3 cup warm water
2 teaspoons granulated sugar
1-1/2 teaspoons active dry yeast
3/4 cup warm milk
3/4 cup plain Greek yogurt or plain, unsweetened, unflavored yogurt
1/4 cup olive oil
4 cups all-purpose flour
1 teaspoon baking powder
1 teaspoon salt
Melted butter for brushing on the tops of the fried naan

You can mix this dough in a stand mixer, or you can mix and knead by hand. Both work about the same, but the stand mixer is less messy!

Naan (and how to make a naanini)

Combine the water, sugar and yeast. Let sit for 5-10 minutes or until the mixture begins to bubble on top

Add in the milk, yogurt, oil, flour, baking powder and salt. Mix until the dough comes together.

If you're using a stand mixer, mix with a dough hook for about five minutes. If you're not using a stand mixer, turn dough out onto lightly floured surface once you've mixed it. Use floured hands to knead the dough until smooth, about 5 minutes. If the dough is very stiff, rinse your hands with warm water and knead with wet hands, so you're mixing in a bit of water as you knead.

Lightly grease a medium-sized bowl with a few quick sprays of cooking oil. Transfer dough to the bowl and cover with plastic wrap. Let rest at room temperature for about an hour until doubled in size.

When ready to cook, divide the dough into ten equal pieces (I use a bench scraper). Roll into balls, then use a rolling pin to roll each piece of dough into a large oval, about 6-inches long and 1/8-inch thick. Keeping it thin will help it form nice bubbles and texture as you fry it up.

Heat a large skillet over medium-high heat. Add some of the olive oil.

Place one piece of the naan on the oiled hot skillet and cook until bubbles form on top, about 2 minutes. While cooking, brush the top with a little oil.

Flip and cook for another 1-2 minutes, until large golden spots appear on the bottom.

Remove from the skillet and wrap in a clean kitchen towel. Repeat with the remaining naan (keep them wrapped in a towel while you work).

Brush each with butter if you'd like, and if you're a garlic fan, use a garlic press and smear garlic and minced parsley on the naan.

How to make a naanini

Making a naanini is a little like making a toasted cheese sandwich, since the idea is to press on it as it's cooking, so the cheese melts and sticks the sandwich contents together. Once you've grilled it, slice it in half. It'll be easier to handle and less will spill out.

You might want to think of these sandwich fillings for your naanini—anything that goes with melted cheese works.

- Sliced chicken or turkey
- Roasted red peppers, drained and patted dry
- Caramelized onions
- Mild cheeses, like Havarti, provolone, paneer (Indian cheese)—or even Brie

Mint chutney works well as a sauce, either spread on the sandwich or to dip it into.

If you want to, mix up some raita (Greek yogurt with minced cucumber, cumin, and mint or cilantro in it) as a dip for your sandwich.

Take two of your naan. Brush butter on the top and bottom naans on one side, then lay down the buttered side of the first naan in a frying pan or grill, set at medium heat. Pile on the toppings and a light coating of sauce, then lay on the top naan, with buttered side up.

As it cooks, press down on the sandwich with a large spatula till the cheese starts to melt. When the sandwich seems stable and "glued" together, use the spatula to carefully turn the sandwich upside down, so the buttered top gets to grill.

Laying a cloche or a pan lid over the top for a few minutes will also get the cheese melting.

When the top and bottom naans are nicely golden

brown, carefully take your sandwich out of the pan or off the grill. Slice in half and enjoy!

Chess Square Cookies
(Shackrutor)

Time: About 1 hour, 45 minutes

Ingredients

1 cup butter, room temperature

1 cup granulated sugar

1 egg, plus 1 egg yolk - mixed together in a small bowl

1 teaspoon vanilla extract

1 1/2 teaspoons baking powder

1/4 teaspoon kosher salt

Chess Square Cookies (Shackrutor)

3 cups all-purpose flour
1/3 cup unsweetened cocoa powder
Set aside for adding to the chocolate mixture:
1 tablespoon cold water
1 tablespoon butter
1 tablespoon softened butter

Instructions

These instructions are for a stand mixer, which blends things more thoroughly, but you can also mix by hand—if you use this method, make sure your final dough is consistently mixed.

In the bowl of your stand mixer, fitted with the paddle attachment, mix together the butter and sugar for 2 minutes.

Add in the egg and the yolk, vanilla, baking powder, and salt and mix for 1 minute until smooth, scraping the sides of the bowl as necessary.

Slowly add in the flour, mixing until just combined.

Divide the dough in half, removing half from the mixing bowl.

Creating the two colors

To the half that's in the mixer (or your mixing bowl) add in the cocoa powder—and also add 1 tablespoon butter, 1 tablespoon sugar and 1 tablespoon cold water—to the remaining dough in the mixing bowl and mix all until incorporated.

Form each dough into a squared-off log, 2- inches square and 6- inches long. Make sure both color blocks are the same size.

Place dough on a baking sheet and cover with cling

wrap. Place dough into the refrigerator to chill for at least 1 hour.

Using a sharp knife, slice the dough into thirds, long-wise. then take each long flat strip and cut into even thirds. If you want your squares to look very precise, use a ruler to measure where you will cut to create three even cuts across the dough.

You will have 9 long strips for each color. Repeat the process with the other colored dough. You will have 18 strips total—each strip about six inches long and of about 2/3 inch square in width.

Lay one strip of vanilla dough, one strip of chocolate, and another strip of vanilla dough on a flat surface next to each other. Top the 3 strips with alternating colors. Repeat this once more, so you have a square log, made up of nine strips. Press the dough strips together tightly, keeping the square shape. Keep a small bowl of warm water near—dip your fingers in and smooth out any cracks. The water will help the "logs" adhere to each other. Repeat this with the remaining dough.

Refrigerate again for at least 30 minutes.

Preheat the oven to 350°F. Line a baking sheet with parchment paper or spray with cooking spray.

Remove the dough from the refrigerator and use a very sharp, non-serrated knife to slice the log into 1/4- inch pieces.

Place the pieces on the baking sheet.

Bake for 10 minutes, or until set. Transfer to a baking rack to cool completely.

Homemade Chai Tea

Ingredients

1 tablespoon black peppercorns

9 3-inch cinnamon sticks, broken into pieces

1 tablespoon whole cloves

1/2 teaspoon fennel seeds

2 tablespoons cardamom

2 tablespoons ground ginger

1 teaspoon turmeric powder

Put all ingredients in a spice or coffee grinder or in a powerful blender, such as a Vitamix.

Grind to a fine powder, then sift to get any chunks out. Store in an airtight container.

To make a batch of chai, then, add 1-1/2 teaspoons of this powder to four cups of boiling water. Add two black tea bags, 1/2 cup of milk or dairy-free alternative, and honey to taste.

Let this mixture boil for about 5 minutes--then let it sit for about 10 minutes so all the ingredients can steep.

Then take out the tea bags, and serve the tea in cups, hot.

If you'd like:

Top off the drink with grated fresh ginger. My editor tops this with a dollop of whipped cream and a few shakes of cinnamon.

Naan the Wiser Playlist

A playlist of chess-based songs, suggested by Laughing Loaf Bakery Mystery fans. Includes 1986's "One Night in Bangkok," from ABBA's *Chess* musical.

Naan the Wiser playlist on Spotify